Dark Secret

Cowboys of Turning Point Ranch Series:
Book 7

AE Moran

The Invisible Publishing Company

Cowboys of Turning Point Ranch Series

Contents

Chapter 1: Ethan

I raise my hand and squint into whipping wind, but it only blows dust in my eyes. The bandana over my face doesn't protect my eyes.

I shake off the dust and try to see the cattle in front of me. They stretch out in a long line.

My brothers flank them in two rows on either side of the herd. Chuck, Wade, Nathan, and Nolan Dewey ride on one side of the herd.

Ben, Jake, Gabe, and Hank Earnhart ride on the left side. That leaves me and Jack Bosch in the back to drive the cattle into the next pasture.

Wade and Jake stop at the gate. The boys have to keep riding back and forth to make sure the cattle don't break out of line in the wind.

Jack and I swing our ropes, yell, and whistle at the cattle to force them to keep pushing face first into the pelting wind. They don't want to go, but they have to.

Chuck and Hank get to the fence. Just a little further and we're done.

I can barely hear Wade and Chuck yelling over the wind, but I already know what they're saying.

As soon as we finish here, we'll pull back to the ranch house. We can't accomplish anything in this windstorm.

Ben and Nathan join the boys at the fence. I'm almost there.

I lower my head, but my hat doesn't protect me, either. I can ride the rest of the way with my eyes closed if I have to.

Another shout makes me look up. The last cattle gallop into the pasture. Jack and I rein our horses back so Ben can swing the gate closed. We're done. Phew!

"Pack it in!" Wade hollers. "Get these horses under cover and head for the house!"

We all turn away, but right at that moment, a menacing crackle sizzles through the air. The sky splits apart and a fork of lightning stabs down to the ground.

It strikes a power pole down on the Turning Point Ranch driveway. The pole explodes and sparks fountain from the transformers holding the lines in place.

A deafening thunderclap goes off a split second later and the cattle squeal behind us. Some of them charge against each other and hit the fence hard enough to jostle the posts in their sockets.

The impact tears the hasp off the gate. It starts to swing open. Ben and I dive off our horses, rush over there, and close it just in time.

More lightning strikes crash all over the ranch, but they all target the power poles. The thunder doesn't let up.

"Get off your horses!" Chuck bellows over the noise. "Get down on the ground! Hurry!"

The others dive off their horses, but we're totally exposed up here on the hilltops. We have nowhere to take shelter.

"Come on!" Wade yells. "We gotta get off the tops!"

"We can't leave this gate open!" I holler back. "The cattle will escape! That's a whole day's work gone! Ben and I will stay up here while you boys ride down to the house and come back in your truck. You can park it across the gate to hold it closed. Then we'll go into town and get a replacement hasp."

He gives me a hard look, compresses his lips, and nods. "I don't like leaving you out here with all this lightning going off."

"We'll stay low against the fence. The lightning will hit the fence first. Go, Wade! You know this is right!"

He clenches his jaw, nods again, and leaves. He and the boys lead their horses down the mountain on foot. It's too dangerous for any of them to ride on horseback.

I wave to Ben. "Get down on the ground—and stay close to the fence."

We both squat down on this side of the gate. Then we sit on the grass and lean our backs against the gate.

The cattle run around in the pasture, kick up their heels, and snort and bawl in fear every time the lightning cracks.

The cattle don't come near the gate or the fence. The stock see the closed gate. They don't realize they could escape if they just hit Ben and me hard enough.

Ben shoots me one of his wild smirks on the side. "This is exciting, isn't it?"

"Don't start enjoying yourself." I squint up at the clouds rolling and churning above our heads. "Power must be off to the rest of the ranch. This is gonna take an eternity to fix."

"We don't have to fix it. The power company will."

I settle in to wait. "It shouldn't take too long for Wade to come back—unless something is wrong at the house."

"Do you ever wonder what our lives would have been like if we never came to live here?" Ben asks out of nowhere.

"No!" I snap. "And you shouldn't be thinking about it, either."

He grins at me. "Why not? I think about it all the time. Don't tell me you aren't grateful."

I look away. "I don't need to think about it. We're here. That's all we need to know."

Fortunately for my sanity, we don't have to talk about it anymore because Wade drives up in his truck just then.

Ben and I move out of the way while Wade pulls his truck right up against the gate.

"Ben and I will go down to the hardware store in town and get the new hasp," I tell him.

"Don't volunteer me for the job!" Ben counters.

"You might as well go," Wade tells him. "You'll just be sitting around in the house with no power if you don't go."

"I can always eat," Ben teases.

I groan and roll my eyes. "Please."

"You can eat when you get back," Wade tells him. "I'm sure the other boys won't have eaten all the food while you're gone."

"I bet they will," he counters.

I push him down the mountain. "You heard the man. We're going. You'll be too fat to ride a horse if you do nothing but sit around all day and eat."

He only laughs. He doesn't give me or Wade any more static about it until we make it back to the ranch house.

The family stands around in the shadowy living room talking about the power outage. Chuck is on his phone with the power company.

"They're already busy trying to deal with the outage," he tells us after he hangs up. "More than a hundred other ranches are all out, too, so we could be stuck like this for a while."

It quickly becomes obvious that there's nothing to do but sit around and wait. I don't have any problem getting Ben to leave after that.

We get into my truck and drive down to Coeur d'Alene. The weather down here is normal. The lightning storm didn't cover this much of the state.

We go into the hardware store and get the hasp. While we're there, I get a phone call from Chuck telling me the electrical fuses in the ranch house and the bunkhouse are all blown.

He talks me through selecting the right ones to replace them. I hang up and head back to the gate hardware section. I turn the corner and see Ben talking to a beautiful young black woman.

Black women are rare in Idaho, so of course he's over there putting on his best charm to sweet-talk her.

She smiles and blushes when he jokes and flirts with her.

She wears her hair in long corn braids with colored ribbons twisted into them. Two small tasteful hoop earrings decorate her earlobes. She doesn't wear any other jewelry.

Her plain jeans, white sneakers, and a white blouse tied at the waist show off her hourglass figure. She has a simple, girl-next-door vibe like she isn't trying to impress anyone with her looks.

She sure is pretty, but I don't interfere. Ben is the lady's man around here and he doesn't have any trouble holding her undivided attention.

I check out a few other pieces of gate hardware while I wait. I see a few different things we might need for the ranch.

I'm just about to call Chuck back and ask him if he wants me to get anything else when Ben says, "This is my brother, Ethan Ingram—and I'm Ben."

I turn around. The young woman is just turning in my direction to smile at me. She flashes me a big, bright, toothy grin and holds out her hand. "It's nice to meet you. I'm Ivy Harper."

I shake her hand, but I keep it formal. I'm not about to start expressing interest in any woman Ben expresses interest in.

He's better looking than I am anyway. He can get any girl he wants. He's proven it more times than I can count.

I don't compete with my brothers for girls. If a girl wants me, she better not be interested in any of my brothers. That's a dealbreaker for me.

I just say, "Nice to meet you." Then I turn to Ben. "We should go."

"Yeah." He grins at her. "Maybe we'll see you around sometime."

She beams at him—and then at me. "Yeah. That would be nice. It's great to see some familiar faces around town."

Ben and I walk away, but not before he shoots her a few more suggestive smiles over his shoulder. I don't turn around to look at her again.

We head for the register. He waits until we turn another corner before he hoots and shakes one hand like he burned himself. "Whoo! She was smoking! Did you see that smile?" He lays his hand on his heart. "I think I'm in love!"

I roll my eyes. "You fall in love every time you take a leak. Leave the girl alone for a change. She's too nice for you."

He points at me. "You see? You thought she was nice, too. Anyway, at least we aren't the only black people in all of Idaho."

"What the hell are you talking about?!" I counter. "You know we aren't."

"Did you know about her? Have you ever seen her before?"

"No, but she could have just moved here. That doesn't mean anything. There is no sign at the state line that says, 'No black people allowed'."

He bursts out laughing. "I think we would have heard by now if there was."

I keep my mouth shut. Now I know he's messing with me.

He can have Ivy if he really wants her. I have more important things to do.

I pull out my wallet while we wait at the register to pay for our supplies. I catch a glimpse of Ivy getting into line at a different register.

She stands facing sideways from us. She sure is pretty in a simple, elegant way. She smiles so genuinely.

I tear my eyes away from her. I'm sure she isn't the only black woman in Idaho. In fact, I know she isn't.

It doesn't matter because I've dated plenty of women of other races, including white, Native American, Latina, and even Middle Eastern.

I really don't care what a woman's race is and I'm not interested in Ivy anyway. I don't know her from a hole in the ground.

The line moves forward. Three people stand between me and the register.

My mind goes back to the situation at the ranch. How long will it take before the power company restores power?

Almost as if that thought makes it happen, a crack of thunder rattles the store windows right then.

Everyone looks up—and my heart stops when a curtain of lightning strikes the city streets right outside the hardware store.

Flashes, forks, and crackles dance beyond the window in a sheet of electricity—and then the thunder hits.

A bone-crushing boom slams into the store and shatters all the front windows. People scream and duck behind the counters.

I wait a fraction of a second too long, and at that moment, a big rig comes barreling down the street from my right.

The truck is driving along at normal speed. It looks like it's driving in a straight line in its lane.

A fork of lightning strikes the hood right outside the hardware store. The truck flips onto its side, skids across the street, and smashes its top right into the store's front wall.

Time slows to a crawl when I see the truck coming closer. I dive behind the counter just as the truck collides with the building.

The collision shakes the walls and vibrates through the floor. More people scream—and then dead silence falls over the store.

Chapter 2: Ivy

I stand up and blink in disbelief at the scene of chaos and destruction all around me.

A massive semi truck blocks light from coming through the hardware store's front windows. It casts the registers in shadow.

Broken glass lies all over the floor along with mortar, bricks, and a bunch of other debris from the crash.

The crash also knocked out power to the store—or maybe the lightning storm did that. None of the registers are working now.

A woman at the next register starts moaning and wringing her hands in despair. "It's blocking the exit! We can't get out! We're trapped in here!"

More murmurs break out up and down the crowd. People get more agitated with every passing minute.

One man raises his voice over the crowd. It's one of the guys I spoke to earlier—but it isn't the charming, athletic, smiling guy with the dreadlocks—Ben, he said his name is Ben. Ben Ingram.

The man who speaks up is Ben's much more muscular, more serious brother—Ethan.

"We aren't trapped in here, folks! Everyone stay calm!" he calls out. "We can get out through the back doors, but we can't go out there now. The lightning is too dangerous. Everybody stay put until the storm passes." He turns to his brother. "Call the Police. You might not be able to get through if they have a lot of other calls, but try anyway."

Ben pulls out his phone and starts tapping on it. He never once argues back. He acts like he's used to Ethan telling him what to do.

A few more people murmur and whisper to each other. An elderly man puts his arm around the woman who panicked earlier. That must be her husband.

Ethan walks over to the overturned semi, paces up and down in front of the windows, and examines the truck from all sides, but he can't get out nor can he see a way to get into the cab to check on the driver. The cab and all the cab windows are outside the store building.

Ethan's boots cowboy boots crunch in all the broken glass. His footsteps sound extra loud in the silence.

He comes back to the register and raises his chin at the young woman standing behind the counter. "Go get the manager and tell whoever it is that we're going to need to find whatever emergency exits or loading dock you have on the other side of this building. We'll need to use another exit to get out of here."

The clerk scampers. I stand there staring at Ethan. He paces back and forth and examines everyone in the crowd with eagle eyes. "Is anyone hurt? Did anyone get hit by flying glass—or anything else?"

A few people shake their heads. He barely glances at me.

His eyes go hard, but his authority calms everyone down. Thank the stars someone level-headed is taking charge of this situation.

He goes back over to Ben. Ben moves the phone away from his mouth. "I'm on hold. They're really busy."

"Hang up," Ethan tells him. "We aren't in any danger here."

Ben hangs up immediately. I'm starting to see a pattern here.

The young clerk comes back with the manager. He's a spidery, bony, middle-aged guy with a greying comb-over.

"We need to find another way out of here," Ethan tells him. "We need an emergency exit or a warehouse loading dock or something like that."

The manager nods. "You can go out through the warehouse. It's right through here." He jerks his thumb toward the back of the store.

Ethan raises his voice to the other customers. "Everyone stay here! I'm going to check on another way to get out of here, but we still can't leave until the storm passes. Stay here. I'll come back and let you know when it's safe to leave the building."

No one argues. He leaves with Ben and the manager. No one says a word until the three men turn out of earshot.

"Good old Ethan," someone remarks behind me. "He's a rock."

I turn around to see who's talking. It's another middle-aged man, but this guy is much bigger, bulkier in the shoulders, and his neck is almost as thick as his skull.

He wears faded jeans, cowboy boots, and an ancient cowboy hat.

"He always was so solid and serious," a woman standing nearby agrees. "He's been like this since he was a little boy."

"It's such a tragedy about his father dying," a different, much thinner man adds. "Those boys learned from the best."

A few other people nod in agreement like they all know everything there is to know about Ben and Ethan.

Ethan comes back a minute later. Ben isn't with him.

Ethan casts another appraising glance over the customers and staff standing around the registers. Nothing has changed since he left.

He stops next to the three people who were just talking about him behind his back.

"Ben is keeping an eye on the sky out back," Ethan announces. "He'll let us know when it's clear to leave. There's too much lightning out there now."

"Thank you, son," the man in the cowboy hat replies.

Ethan levels the guy with a hard look. "What are you doing catting around town in the middle of the workday? Shouldn't you be out there saying bad words to your tractor?"

The guy bursts out in deep-chested laughter. "I could ask you the same question. Shouldn't you be at work?"

Ethan holds up a gate hasp and a handful of fuses. "I am at work. The lightning took out the power, so Ben and I came in here to get supplies. It beats sitting around in the dark."

The other guy nods, and just then, Ben comes back. "It looks clear—clear enough for everyone to get around to the parking lot and into their cars." He points to the north. "You'll all have to go around the block over there. The street out front is completely blocked by emergency vehicles."

Ethan raises his voice again. "Everyone follow me! I'll show you were to go."

He leads the way into the back. I catch Ben smiling at me when I walk past him, but all other eyes remain fixed on Ethan.

He leads the crowd through the aisles and through a set of swinging doors into the warehouse attached to the back of the store.

We find the manager standing by the loading dock roll-up doors. The wind and lightning have died down.

Ethan pulls out his wallet, counts some cash into the manager's hand for his purchases, and leads the way down a set of stairs next to the dock to the ground.

He keeps going, turns the corner to the other side of the building, and waves toward the parking lot. "You can all get into your cars and go home. The store won't open for business again until they clean up the mess and turn the power back on."

Everyone separates to their cars. I have to pass him to get to mine. He makes a split second of eye contact with me, dips his chin once to nod at me, and walks away.

He and Ben get into a sleek, black pickup truck. Ethan gets behind the wheel. They pull out onto the road and turn left to head north before they pass out of sight.

Chapter 3: Ivy

I pull my car into the driveway and peer through the windshield at a curved wooden sign overhead. It reads, *Turning Point Ranch.* I've come to the right place.

I pause there and check the file on the passenger seat. The name on the account is Turning Point Ranch. The ranch owner is listed as Turning Point Ranch Trust.

The contacts for the account are Wade Crenshaw, Ava Crenshaw, Nolan Dewey, and Chuck Keller. I don't know any of those people.

Wade and Ava are probably married. They must be the legal owners of the ranch. Nolan and Chuck must be high-level employees.

I drive the rest of the way to the ranch house. It's a huge palatial mansion with two enormous wings branching off the main central section.

A bunch of vehicles sit in the driveway. Most of them are passenger cars.

I take my account files and my briefcase, get out of the car, and go knock on the door. It takes a while before someone comes to answer.

A middle-aged lady with dyed brown hair opens the door and frowns at me. "Can I help you?"

I hold out my hand to her. "You must be Mrs. Crenshaw. I'm Ivy Harper. I'm the representative for Mighty River Power Company. I'm here to discuss the repairs to your power supply."

She bursts into a huge smile. "Oh, of course! Come on in. The boys are all at work, but you can take a seat until they come back. They can tell you more than I can."

I follow her inside. "Who do you mean by, 'the boys'? The account lists Wade, Nolan, and Chuck as the contacts. Is that who you mean?"

She nods. "They're my sons, but the rest of the boys can tell you just as much about what needs to be repaired and everything." She waves me toward the living room. "Take a seat. I'll get Ava for you."

I stop dead in my tracks. "You aren't Ava?"

She bursts out laughing. She has a warm, cheerful, easy-going smile and sparking dark eyes. "No, sweetie. I'm Camille. Ava is my daughter. She runs the ranch on the business side." She waves me toward the couches. "Just wait here. I'll explain everything when I get back."

She starts walking away. I turn to the couches. Four other women sit there.

One holds a baby boy on her lap. The little guy can barely hold his head up and he keeps his fist jammed into his mouth the whole time. He stares up at me with huge, soft brown eyes.

An old woman with frizzy white hair sits next to the mother. The old lady won't stop beaming at everyone. A young, brown-haired woman sits on the other couch.

The woman standing next to her is a short, petite, Chinese woman with a no-nonsense, direct look. She sticks out her hand to me. "Nice to meet you. Welcome to Turning Point. I'm Liza."

"Um...thanks. I'm Ivy Harper. I'm with the power company." I start to look around—and freeze for the second time when I see a bunch of pictures on the mantle shelf above the fireplace.

All the pictures up there are family photos—and Ben and Ethan are in them.

I point at the biggest one and open my mouth to ask, but the words won't come. What are they doing in a family photograph.....with all these people?

Most of the people in that picture are white—but two of the men are Native American. One is a huge, strapping, dark-skinned guy with long black hair and chiseled, brutal features.

The other is a much shorter, light-skinned, almost Asian-looking guy with short hair and a round, moon-shaped, almost cherubic smile.

Just then, Camille comes back with a tall, blonde, bombshell of a woman wearing jeans and a tight plaid button-up shirt.

"This is my daughter Ava," Camille begins. "She can tell you all about the damage from the lightning strikes." Camille frowns at me. "Is something wrong?"

I gulp to get my voice working. "What are they doing here? Why are Ben and Ethan in your family photographs?"

I realize too late how bad that sounds. I shouldn't be demanding answers about someone else's family business.

The sight of those men shocks me so much that the words fall out of my mouth.

"Oh, you know about Ben and Ethan?" Camille walks around me to look at the picture, too. "They're adopted. They're my adopted sons along with....." She points out each person one after the other. "Chuck Keller, Wade, Nathan, Jake, Gabe, and Jack Bosch. That's Nolan Dewey, Ava's husband, and Hank Earnhart, my daughter Emma's husband."

The young woman on the other couch raises her hand, waves, smiles at me. "Hi."

"This is Hank's grandmother, Rosa Pendergrass, my son Nathan's wife, Liza Donahue, and this is my daughter-in-law, Grace Adams, Wade's wife, and their son, Eli." Camille frowns at me. "Are you sure you don't want to sit down? Would you like something to drink?"

"No, no!" I shake myself back to my senses. "I'm sorry. I didn't mean to be rude. I met Ben and Ethan in town—at the hardware store. I just didn't think....I didn't know...."

Camille bursts into a grin. "Most people around here already know about the boys. You're one of the few who doesn't. We adopted all four boys out of foster care when they were little. They've been living with us ever since." She laughs. "Sometimes I even forget they are adopted."

Ava sits down on the arm of the couch next to the Grace. "What do you need to know about the damage?"

"Oh, right!" I pounce on my briefcase, open it, and start taking out the case files for the ranch. "Well, we have reports from the district transformers and electrical relays, so we know which junctions need repair. We need you—or somebody associated with the trust—to sign off on permission for our repair crews to come onto the property and make repairs."

"I can do that," Ava replies. "Is that all you need?"

I flip open a few more folders. "You see, it appears the ranch's existing infrastructure was put in place when your power needs were much less than they are now. You've added another structure........that house up there....."

I point through the windows across the backyard to the house up the hill. It sits apart from the main ranch house.

"That's the bunkhouse," Camille tells me. "My late husband Tom and I had the house built for our hired men—but that was decades ago. We got approval from the county to build the house. They never said anything about upgrading the power supply."

"You have to admit, though, Mama, that the power draw for the bunkhouse is much higher now than it was before," Emma cuts in. "No one has lived there for years besides Hank and Nolan and they always went out to work for most of the day. They came down here for all their meals. They never cooked up there or spent any time there—and then Hank lived there alone after Nolan moved down here. Now Tati and I are up there all day every day." She waves to the old woman across the living room from her. "The bunkhouse uses a lot more power than it used to."

"You have to admit the main ranch house uses a lot more power now than it did back then, too," Ava points out. "We have the computer lab and all of us are grown up with phones, computers, and other electronics. There are a lot more people living here and we aren't kids anymore."

"Actually, it isn't just the two houses," I interrupt. "It appears from a grid layout of the property that you have power draws on multiple sites all over the acreage."

"Those power sources work the water pumps that supply water to our stock herd," Ava tells me. "We need those."

"Yes, of course, I understand," I tell her. "I'm just saying that we need to upgrade your infrastructure to compensate for the greater load draw. That's all I'm saying. You would have suffered a breakdown eventually even if this lightning storm hadn't damaged your infrastructure. We might as well upgrade you while the repair crews are already on the property. They can kill two birds with one stone."

She raises both hands and gets to her feet. "I think you better talk to Wade and Chuck about this."

"But you already said you could sign off on the repair crew access," I point out.

"I could have if it was just for the repairs."

"Why can't you sign off on this, too? You're listed as a contact for the power account. These upgrades need to happen sooner rather than later. Delaying them will only cause problems in the future."

"Just talk to Wade and Chuck about this. They can tell me if they want me to sign off on it."

I frown at her. "I don't understand why you need their approval."

"They make the decisions about what happens to the ranch." She raises her hands a little higher. "Just ask them. That's just the way we do things around here. None of us can make that decision without running it by them."

I still don't understand, but just then, a vehicle door slams in the driveway outside.

Ava turns away. "It sounds like they're coming in now. You can talk to them about it and tell them what you just told me."

I don't know what to think about this. I've never encountered a situation like this before. There is nothing in the account that indicates that Ava has any less authority to make this decision than anyone else.

Wade and Chuck are her brothers—and Chuck is her adoptive brother. Does that have something to do with this?

Then I remember. Ben and Ethan are Ava's adoptive brothers, too.

My head spins when I think about all the implications. These people adopted Ben and Ethan out of foster care—and the Crenshaws adopted Jack and Chuck out of foster care, too.

What must it have been like for Ben and Ethan to grow up with white parents, white siblings, and even two Native American siblings?

I catch a glimpse of Liza standing across the room. She's Chinese, married to a white man, the sister-in-law of all these adopted brothers.

This family is such a melting-pot of personalities—and yet none of them seems to think this is in any way out of the ordinary.

Those people in town didn't seem to think it was out of the ordinary, either. They all knew Ben and Ethan. Those people made it sound like they had known the Crenshaws since Ben and Ethan were little boys.

Then I remember the second man talking about their father dying. The guy made it sound recent. They must have been talking about the Crenshaw family's late father—that strong-looking man in the pictures.

All the Crenshaws stand with their arms around each other in the picture. Ethan has one arm around his father and the other around a thick-set, burly, ferocious-looking guy. I think Camille said his name was Nathan.

The others all hold onto each other. None of them looks like they even notice that four of their brothers come from other races. I've never seen a family like this before.

Chapter 4: Ivy

I jump out of my skin when the front door of the Turning Point ranch house opens.

Ava goes over there and meets all the Crenshaw boys coming through the door—all except Gabe and Jake. They aren't here.

I get an eyeful of these men in living color while she explains everything to them that I just explained to her.

I stand up and turn around. Ben grins and strides right up to me with his hand out. "Great to see you again, Ivy. Welcome to our humble abode."

"Don't listen to a word he says!" Jack calls from the back of the group. "He doesn't even know the meaning of the word, 'humble'."

"Of course I do," Ben yells back. "It means, 'not proud'."

"Like I said," Jack returns.

Ethan hangs back and barely nods at me. He says, "Hello," and that's all.

Wade and Chuck come into the living room to talk to me. Wade takes Eli out of Grace's arms and Wade bounces his knees up and down while we talk.

"So what are the upgrades you need to do?" he asks.

I give him the briefest possible summary of the transformer up-grades that will modulate the new power load. I also outline the time-line for the repairs.

"So that will take longer to complete than just repairing what we already have," Chuck interrupts.

"Yes, that's true, but it will avoid breakdowns, outages, and the need for further repair in the future," I point out.

"We haven't had any breakdowns, outages, or needed any repairs so far," Wade cuts in. "How much will the upgrades cost the ranch?"

"I have the cost breakdown here." I bend over to take the docu-ments out of my briefcase.

Wade plays with the baby while he waits and kisses him behind the ear to make him laugh. Grace stands up and jerks her thumb toward the stairs. "I'm just going to....." She doesn't finish her sentence.

He nods at her. "Go."

She takes off without another word of explanation. I hold out the documents, but Chuck is the one who takes them.

He reads the first page and then flips to the second one. Wade doesn't look at them at all. He keeps playing with his baby son.

"So we would be liable for the repairs either way—whether we upgrade or not," Chuck points out. "We're liable for all the damage inside the property line."

"Yes—technically—but you should be able to recover that from your homeowner's insurance provider."

"What about the upgrade?" Wade asks.

I shuffle my feet. "I don't know about that. You would have to check with your provider."

"We'll need to discuss that and look into it," Chuck tells me. "We can't decide on this right now."

"I would suggest that you sign off on the repairs either way," I tell him. "The repair crews have a busy schedule. You want to schedule them to come out as soon as possible even if you don't upgrade. The longer you wait, the longer you have to wait to do the repairs."

The two men exchange glances. No one else offers any other input.

I sense everyone standing around listening to our conversation. I would normally push a lot harder for them to accept the upgrade.

It is part of my job to get our customers to accept these necessary improvements when the power company doesn't think the existing infrastructure is good enough.

I don't seem to be able to do that here. It is Wade's and Chuck's decision whether to accept this upgrade.

They're both making so many good arguments against it that I can't bring myself to flex my non-existent expertise by insisting on it.

They're right that their current infrastructure has been holding up pretty well. Who knows how much longer Turning Point Ranch could go on with no problems?

"If we schedule the regular repairs now, can we change our minds and add the upgrade to the schedule before the repair crew comes out—just to give us time to look into this?" Wade asks.

"Sure!" I exclaim. "You just need to get in touch with the power company and change the order on the repair schedule."

"All right. We'll do that." He looks around at all my paperwork scattered everywhere. "What do we need to sign?"

Ava appears out of nowhere. "I'll take care of it. You boys better go get changed for dinner. Come with me, Ivy. I'll sign off on it."

She leads the way through the living room to a hallway heading to the west wing of the house.

The brothers and the other women split up and leave in different directions. Wade disappears upstairs with his son.

Hank sits down with Emma. His grandmother leaves and starts making her way up the hill to the bunkhouse.

She's a frail old lady who hobbles when she walks, but she still makes it up there just fine.

I don't see where the others go. Ava shows me down the hall and turns off into a large, brightly lit office with a dozen computers standing around on different desks and workstations.

Nolan follows us into the room, but he doesn't get involved in the sign-off process. He goes to one of the computers and starts working on it.

I hand Ava the repair agreement. She puts it on one of the workstations and reads it over in detail before she signs it.

She smiles when she hands it back. "There you go. Was there anything else you needed from us?"

"That's all. The repair crew will get in touch with you before they come out to the property. They'll let you know if you need to partition off certain areas of the property so no people or livestock are in any danger while the crews work."

Ava nods. "Thanks. Come on. I'll walk you out."

I follow her back to the living room Only Camille and Emma are even still here. Everyone else is gone.

I shake hands with both of them, say my goodbyes, and Ava accompanies me to the door.

I turn to her on the porch. "Bye," I tell her. "It was really nice meeting your family."

"Thanks for being so understanding. I'm sure I'll see you around."

"I'm sure you will." I smile at her. "See ya."

"Bye," she replies.

I turn toward the driveway when, at that moment, a catastrophic lightning bolt shoots out of the sky.

That one bolt hits a power pole right in front of the house, explodes the transformer on top of the pole, and splits the pole down one side.

I can only stand and stare in shock when the pole topples and smashes right on top of my car. It caves in the roof and completely implodes the driving compartment.

That lightning strike is only the first of many. Countless forks erupt out of the sky. They dance all over the countryside with no sign of slowing down.

Camille, Jack, and Chuck materialize behind me. Ava is still standing next to me with her jaw on the floor.

"Wow," Jack murmurs. "That didn't go well."

I gulp. My car is completely destroyed.

Camille comes to my rescue and grabs my arm. "Come inside, darlin'. You can't drive back to town in that."

"You can't drive back to town at all with this lightning going on," Chuck points out. "You better stick around until it dies down."

I turn around and see Nolan and Ethan standing behind the others. Neither of them get involved in the conversation, but they can both see my car completely squashed under that pole.

"Don't worry, Ivy," Camille tells me. "One of the boys will drive you back to town."

Chuck pulls out his phone. "I'm calling the power company. They have to remove the lines before any of us can get out of the driveway."

"You better stay for dinner, at least," Camille adds. "It's already late and this could take a while. Come inside and sit down."

I stumble back inside the house just as the rest of the family shows up. The guys have all showered and changed into clean clothes. They don't smell as dusty and sweaty now.

They gather around, look at the power pole lying across my car, and discuss the recent lightning storms at length.

I sink onto the couch. Ben comes over and sits down next to me. "Hey, this could be a good thing, right? When was the last time you had a home-cooked meal?"

I make a face and try not to notice him flirting with me again. "Too long, actually."

"See? This is a sign from God."

"It isn't a sign from God for you to move in on the power company rep," Nathan snaps from across the room. "Don't make me get out the horse whip."

Ben smirks at him and then at me. "He only says that because he loves me."

"I love you enough to drive you off with a stick." Nathan turns to me. "Don't hesitate to tell him to go stick his head in a bucket of ice water."

"I don't think it's his head that needs to get stuck in a bucket of ice water," I tell him.

The whole room explodes with laughter. Some of the other guys come over to Ben, grab him by the shoulders, shake him, and give him a hard time about what I said.

He won't stop blushing, but he's laughing too hard to take it personally.

He raises both hands and gets to his feet. "I'm just going to back away....very slowly.....nice and easy....."

The other guys laugh—all except Ethan. He watches from a distance and remains silent. Is he always this reserved or is he only acting this way because I'm here?

Ben gets pulled into conversation with his brothers. Liza comes back to the couches, sits down next to me, and starts asking me when I moved to Coeur d'Alene.

"I just moved here a few months ago," I tell her. "I moved from North Carolina."

"What made you move?" Emma asks from the other couch.

I shrug. "I just needed a change of scenery. I was born and raised in Greenville. I lived in North Carolina all my life. I guess I wanted to see what it was like out in the Wild West."

More laughter breaks out when the brothers hear me. Then Camille calls us to the table.

They seat me in the middle of the table between Jack on one side and Hank on the other. All the couples sit together, so Emma sits on Hank's other side.

I wind up sitting directly across from Ben. He doesn't stop smiling at me through the whole meal.

Ethan sits at the far end of the table next to his mother. He's farther away—almost far enough away for me to ignore and for him to ignore me, but I still sense him watching my every move.

Chapter 5: Ethan

Everyone talks, laughs, jokes, and shoots snide remarks back and forth during dinner. I find my attention always going back to Ivy even though she sits four places away from me.

I shouldn't let myself get interested in her—like I don't have enough problems already.

The attention she's getting from Ben is enough to put her out of my reach—and I'm not even interested in her.

It isn't because she's one of the very few black women I've met in Idaho. That has nothing to do with it.

She's personable, warm, and interacts easily with everyone. I don't see her acting any differently toward Ben than she acts toward anyone else.

She doesn't respond to his flirtations even though he makes it so over-the-top obvious what he's doing.

I make a point not to look in her direction unless the conversation calls for it. Most of it centers around the recent lightning storms.

Then she, Ben, and the others talk about the semi truck crashing into the hardware store. She doesn't say anything about me helping everyone get out of the building.

Ben is the one who tells everyone that I basically took over the scene.

"It was great," Ivy exclaims. "It calmed everyone down. The other customers appreciated it. They said so when you went into the warehouse to check out the other exit."

I concentrate on my food. She better not be trying to start something with me when Ben is already paying her so much attention.

It's my turn to help clean up the kitchen after dinner. I ask my mom for permission to leave the table while the others sit around shooting the breeze.

I go into the kitchen and start cleaning up the pots and pans my mom and the girls used to make dinner. I'm halfway through the first sink load of dishes when Liza and Nathan join me to help out.

Ivy comes over to the kitchen counter. "Can I help?"

"No way," Liza tells her. "You're the guest of honor."

Ivry makes a face. "I'm only here because my car got wrecked. There is no honor in that."

Liza and Nathan laugh. I keep washing the dishes. My mom comes over next. "The repair crew just left, Ivy. They say it's safe for someone to drive you back to town."

"Get Ben to do it," Nathan replies over his shoulder.

"You don't actually think it's a good idea for him to be alone with her, do you?" Liza counters. "He might not survive."

Now it's my turn to laugh. Camille leaves us there and yells up the stairs for Ben to come down, but he doesn't answer.

"I don't know where he went," she mutters when she rejoins us. "He just disappeared."

"It's self-preservation," Liza teases.

"Well, someone has to drive her home. Ethan, you can do it."

I just say, "Yes, Ma'am," and start rinsing and drying my hands on a towel.

I can drive Ivy back to town as well as anyone can. It doesn't mean anything because she doesn't mean anything.

She goes around saying goodbye and thanking everyone. The few people still in the living room gather around and follow us to the door.

I grab my keys, wallet, and phone, and open the passenger door for her so she can get into my truck. Then I start driving down the mountain.

"Your family is really great," she remarks as soon as we pull out of the driveway.

"They're the best," I tell her. "The old man was a rock. We lost a lot when we lost him."

She cocks her head to one side. "That's interesting. Some of the customers at the hardware store said the same thing about you."

I don't take my eyes off the road. "If I am, it's because I learned from the best."

"That's what they said. It's really beautiful how close your family is."

"We're all we've ever had. We wouldn't be much of a family if we weren't close."

"Not many families are as close as you are," she points out. "You must realize that."

"I do, but this is all I've ever known—so it's normal to me."

I feel her studying me from the side. What does she think when she looks at me?

I don't care what she thinks. She isn't part of my life and she isn't going to be.

"What was it like—growing up with the Crenshaws?" she asks.

"It was wonderful. It was perfect. I couldn't ask for better."

"Do you remember anything from your life before you went to live there?"

I shrug that away. I don't take the bait. "Not much. I don't usually think about it. I have my family—and I've always had Ben. I don't really need anything else. The Crenshaws are the only family I've ever had. I don't have any other."

She settles deeper into her seat and gazes out at the dark landscape. "It's so interesting. I wonder if the others remember anything."

"Chuck does. I know he does."

Her head whips around. "He does? How do you know?"

"Because I was already living with the Crenshaws when they adopted him. He's older than I am. He's even older than Wade. Chuck remembers a lot more than I do. It's a shame, too. It would be better if he didn't."

"Why?"

"Because he got really badly abused. That's why he went into the foster system. His parents were drug addicts who abused him. They almost killed him—and they did kill his older brother. Then they OD'ed in the house. The Police found Chuck alone in the house with three bodies and wounds and bruises all over him. He went through hell before he came to live with us. It took him a long time to get over it. That's why he is the way he is."

"Wow," she breathes. "That sounds awful."

"It was. He had a hard time, but he always treated us well. He loved it at the Crenshaws—and he still does. He never looked back. He just has his own demons to fight—but he's a good man—one of the best."

I feel her studying me even more closely. I don't turn around to see her reaction. I really don't care.

I only have to explain this stuff to her because she's new in the area. Everyone else around here already knows about Chuck, Jack, Ben, and me. We don't have to explain anything to anyone.

"How did you and Ben wind up in the foster system?" she asks.

"Some thieves broke into our house and killed our parents in a robbery gone wrong."

"Do you remember that?"

"No, Ben and I were both asleep at the time. The neighbors heard gunshots and called the Police. They were the ones who woke me up. It was all over by then."

"How long were you in foster care?"

"I think it was about a month. You would have to ask my mom. She can tell you exactly. The social worker contacted the Crenshaws as soon as we went into the system. I don't remember anything about that. In my mind, I went from my old house to the Crenshaws with no break."

"That's incredible," she breathes. "The Crenshaws sound like angels."

"They are. Ask any of the boys. The old man was a saint—and Mama still is. She's the best mother that ever lived."

I pull into town. This trip is almost over.

Ivy gives me directions to her apartment. It's a duplex in a nice neighborhood.

She gives me a full, bright, beaming smile when I pull up to the curb. "Would you like to come in?"

"I better not. I have to drive all the way back home and get some sleep for work tomorrow."

I get out of the driver's seat and open her door for her. "Good night," I tell her.

She won't stop smiling at me. "Good night. Thank you for driving me—and for the conversation. I'm really glad I met you."

I see her looking at me like that—and no one could mistake the implications of her inviting me in. I just say, "Good night again," and shut the passenger door so she gets the message.

I walk her as far as the door and stand there until she goes inside. I keep my distance so she knows this is strictly professional. I'm not walking her to the door to imply anything.

She smiles at me one more time, shuts the door, and I go back to my truck, turn the ignition, and drive all the way back to the ranch.

Everyone is already asleep in bed with the lights off by the time I get there.

I go to my room, get in bed, and put Ivy Harper as far out of my mind as possible. She might be interested in me, but it will never go any further than that.

Whatever it is she wants from me, it is never going to happen—not in a million years.

Chapter 6: Ethan

I rev up my chainsaw and squint through my safety glasses as I cut up the old power pole lying across the driveway.

The boys drive back and forth cleaning up the mess from last night's lightning storm. Nolan drives up in his truck with Hank in the passenger seat.

They went up to the top pastures to make sure the cattle are all still fenced in. They must be because neither Hank nor Nolan acts like the top herds are any big emergency we have to go deal with.

We have enough to clean up with power lines down and the repair crews scheduled to come in two weeks. I still don't know what Wade and Chuck will decide about upgrading our infrastructure.

At least we still have power to the ranch house. That's the best we can hope for until the crew comes out to do all the repairs.

I don't have to talk to any of the boys as long as I'm using the chainsaw. Ben, Nathan, and Jack finish whatever they're doing and come over to stack up the log rounds I've just cut up.

I work my way down the pole and leave the ruined transformer lying there on the ground. The power company is supposed to remove it. It's too heavy for me to lift anyway.

Chuck drives over in his truck just as I switch off the saw. He throws a length of chain around the transformer and uses his truck to drag the hunk of useless metal off to one side where it won't block the driveway.

We all gather around Wade's truck to hear what he wants us to do next. "Nathan, you and Ethan go over to Eastwood and see if Gabe needs help with anything. You can come and get us if you need more people. Hank and Nolan, you go over to Iron Mountain and touch base with Jake."

"Haven't you already touched base with him?" Ben asks. "Can't you get him and Gabe on the phone and ask if they need help with anything?"

"Believe or not, I do have a brain and I can think of these things as well as you can," Wade returns. "I already tried calling both of them and I can't raise either of them on the phone because the local mobile network is down. Do you honestly think I would send you over there if I could talk to them on the phone?"

Ben raises both hands in surrender. "It was just a question."

Wade pretends to ignore him. "Chuck and I are going back to the house to hammer out this business with the power company and the upgrades they want us to do. We have a phone consultation with our insurance provider, so we should be able to make a decision as soon as we hear their answer. If they go for it, we'll need to scramble to get ready for the upgrades."

"What do you want me and Ben to do?" Jack asks.

Ben swats him in the shoulder. "Don't ask him that! He might have forgotten all about us. Then we would have gotten the afternoon off."

"Since when are you so lazy?" Nathan snaps. "You're gonna ruin your reputation around here if you keep pulling shit like that."

"I'm just messing around," Ben counters. "Jesus, where is you boys' sense of humor lately?"

"He got lazy when he lost his marbles over the power company rep," Hank chimes in. "His brain turned to mush the minute he laid eyes on her."

Ben laughs. "I'm not that whipped. You gotta admit, though. I had her wrapped around my little finger."

"She had you wrapped around her little finger, you mean," Chuck corrects. "She told you to soak your pecker in a bucket of ice water. It didn't sound like she was falling for you nearly as hard as you fell for her."

Ben laughs again and he actually blushes this time. "I didn't fall for her. She isn't really my type anyway."

"Of course not," Nathan replies. "She's too smart for you."

Ben winces. "Ouch! A guy can be nice to a lady without it turning into something."

"Any guy other than you might be able to do that," Jack tells him. "Don't think we didn't see you flirting with her. You were practically drooling over her."

"No, I wasn't!" Ben fires back. "She's nice and I was trying to be nice back. That's all."

Wade turns to me. "Did anything happen when you drove her home?"

"Nope," I tell him. "I just dropped her off and left."

"Of course nothing happened," Nathan adds. "Ethan is a monk. He doesn't get involved with women. He doesn't even see them."

Jack claps me on the shoulder. "When are you gonna get your first girlfriend, big guy?"

"Just as soon as you pull your head out of your ass and stop being such an immature prick," I tell him.

Wade raises his hands. "Okay, that's enough. Leave the man alone. I'm sure he can handle his private affairs as well as the rest of us. Now get back to work and quit screwing around. Ethan, go with Nathan. The rest of you know what to do. Jack and Ben, come with me."

I leave so I don't hear what Wade tells Jack and Ben to do. I don't want to be around when Wade and Chuck deal with the insurance company, either.

Nathan and I get into his truck. He drives us over to Eastwood to check in with Gabe.

"Don't listen to the boys," he tells me on the way over there. "They don't mean anything by it. If you don't want to get involved with anyone, no one is gonna make you."

I shrug it off without looking at him. "It's no skin off my nose. You boys can say whatever you want. I'm not gonna change the way I do things."

He studies me on the side. "She is a nice girl."

I pretend to look out the side window at the countryside rolling past. "Sure. She's great."

"You could do a lot worse," he points out.

"It doesn't matter because Ben wants her."

"You just heard him say he doesn't."

I shrug that away, too. "It doesn't matter if he does or he doesn't because he already expressed an interest in her. She turned his head. That's enough to take her off the table as far as I'm concerned."

He looks away and clucks his tongue. "It doesn't have to be like that. If he really isn't interested, then you have no reason not to."

"It doesn't matter because I'm not interested in her. He can have her. Anyone can have her."

"You aren't interested in anyone," he mumbles.

"That's my business, isn't it?"

"Yeah. It is."

The conversation dies when he pulls into the driveway at Eastwood. I'm perfectly happy to put the whole subject out of my mind, but I have no choice but to pay attention when Nathan stops his car in the driveway.

Ivy stands next to a different car parked next to Gabe's truck. She's talking to him, smiling at him, and he laughs at something she says.

She's wearing a neat, crisp, beige business suit, a deep navy-blue blouse, and matching beige pumps.

She wore more casual clothes when she came to Turning Point. She looks much fancier here.

Her outfit doesn't quite fit with the surroundings. She looks out of place on a ranch—but she still looks down-to-earth, elegant, and painfully appealing.

She still wears the same colored ribbons braided into her hair. They create a startling contrast to her outfit.

Does she ever change her hairstyle? Is it possible those braids are her real hair? I can't think of any other explanation.

"Well, what do you know?" Nathan murmurs. "It's a small world after all."

I clench my teeth. I don't want to see her. I don't want to talk to her, but it looks like I have to, especially when Nathan gets out of the truck to go over there.

I have to do the same thing, but I make up my mind on the way not to engage with her at all.

She turns and bursts into one of her glorious smiles when she sees us. Nathan walks right up to her and shakes hands. "Look who's here," he exclaims. "Why am I not be surprised to find you here?"

She blushes and her eyes dart to me. "I'm visiting all the ranches in the area to schedule repairs." She checks the paperwork in her arms. "I'm going to Iron Mountain Ranch next. Your brother Jake is listed as the contact there—but the ranch is still listed as owned by your family trust."

Nathan nods. "Yet. We keep it all in the family here." He turns to Gabe. "Wade couldn't reach you on the phone. He sent us over to see if you need any help with anything."

"Yeah, I do," Gabe replies. "Some of the power poles fell across my fences. I moved my stock to other pastures, but I need help putting the fences back up."

"We'll take a look." Nathan turns back to Ivy. "Were you done here or do you still need him?"

She laughs and blushes like he just made a sexual innuendo or something. "I'm done with him. You can have him."

Nathan grins and she grins back—and then she smiles at me. She's still smiling at all of us when she heads for her car and pulls open the passenger door.

This is a different car, of course. The other one got destroyed when the power pole fell on top of it.

This one is a glossy silver sedan with a rental company sticker in the windshield's upper left corner. That explains it.

She bends over to put all her paperwork on the passenger seat. Her skirt shows off her figure from the side, but she doesn't realize it. She bends over facing the car, so it isn't like she's pointing her ass at us to be suggestive.

She stands up, shuts the door, smiles at us, says, "See you all later," and climbs into the driver's seat. She smiles at us one last time through the windshield.

Gabe and Nathan both wave and she waves back before she reverses and drives off.

"How do you know her?" Gabe asks as soon as she leaves.

"She's handling the repairs at the ranch," Nathan replies. "She got stranded there for dinner last night after a power pole fell on her car and crushed it. Ben couldn't stop yapping at her heels the whole time and then he vanished when it was time to drive her home. Now he wants us all to forget it ever happened and think he was never interested in her."

Gabe laughs. "He needs to stick his head in a bucket of cold water. She's too nice for him."

"That's what she told him." Nathan jerks his thumb over his shoulder. "Show us these fences and let's get started. We might need to call in the other boys to help us out."

I get back into Nathan's truck. Gabe loads up in his and we follow Gabe up the hill to the top of the ranch.

We have to park lower than the fence in question and walk the rest of the way. Maybe, just maybe, we can all stop talking about and thinking about Ivy Harper at least for a few hours.

Chapter 7: Ivy

I pull up my new rental car in front of the grocery store. I make sure to check the sky before I get out. I don't want to get caught in another lightning storm like I did at the hardware store.

At least the power company's insurance provider didn't give me any static about getting me a rental to replace my old car.

The sky is perfectly blue with a few fluffy white clouds. That's all. I'm safe for now.

I grab my purse, climb out, and go inside. I'm off work, so I'm wearing casual clothes instead of my business suit.

I see a few people I recognize—both from my recent power company assessments and from the hardware store accident.

Everyone smiles and greets me. I might still be new in town, but people act friendly toward me. I could get used to this.

I head for the produce aisle, load up my basket, and then head for the meats. I'm just putting some ground beef in my basket when none other than four of the Crenshaws come around the corner.

I stop when I see Chuck, Jack, Ben, and Ethan coming toward me. They all pause and slow down when they see me.

Then Jack bursts into a grin and picks up the pace again. "We really can't get rid of you, can we?"

I have to laugh. "Hi, guys. What brings you here? Don't tell me you're buying beef retail."

"Not beef, but everything else," Ben tells me. "We order our groceries in bulk. We're just here to pick up our supplies for the month." He points to the swinging doors leading into the back. "The warehouse just happens to be near the meat section."

I nod. "Of course. That makes sense when you live so far away."

"We rescheduled our repairs," Chuck tells me. "We're going with the upgrade."

I beam at him. "That's great! I'm pleased."

"The insurance is forking out for it, so it was a no-brainer in the end." He turns to the others. "I'll go tell Milo we're here."

He splits off into the back and leaves me alone with Jack, Ben, and Ethan.

Jack and Ben pass the time of day and make jokes about my purchases. Ethan doesn't say a word through our whole conversation.

I eventually excuse myself to continue with my shopping. The three of them go into the back to meet up with Chuck.

I don't think about it again until I get to the register. The Crenshaw boys show up at the same time, but they don't have any purchases.

Chuck carries a printed invoice in his hand. The boys must have already loaded up their goods in their trucks. Now they just have to pay for everything.

I find myself studying the four of them while we wait our turns in line. They are such powerful, well-adjusted men.

They talk to other people in the line who obviously know them and their family. Jack and Ben laugh and joke around with people.

Chuck and Ethan always keep it serious, but they still act personable and don't have any problem talking to those around them.

They are also super polite to the staff. The store manager comes over to talk to Chuck about something. They obviously know each other well.

Chuck talks to him easily. Chuck doesn't act harsh or menacing. He never does even though he's always so serious.

It's a fitting testament to Tom's and Camille's legacy that these men are such an integral part of the local community. No one treats them as anything but men who grew up here, went to school here, and know everybody.

I hate to think what these four men would have turned into without the Crenshaws' intervention. No wonder they all think so highly of Tom and Camille.

I never met Tom, but I do know Camille. I can see Tom's influence stamped into all four of these men—and all the rest of their grown children.

My turn comes at the register. The four Crenshaws are in a different line. I have to turn around to face the register so I can unload my groceries.

My mind drifts back to the repairs. I should follow up on the Turning Point repair job. I should make sure everything is in place and that the repair crew has everything they need to make the upgrades.

I'm just taking my veggies out of my basket when a man strides to the front of the store. He's wearing a long black trench coat over torn jeans, untied work boots, and a stained T-shirt.

Before anyone even realizes what's happening, he pulls an automatic rifle from under his trench coat and fires it into the ceiling.

Four more men in trench coats do the same thing, pivot to the front of the store, and pull identical guns.

"Nobody move!" the first guy bellows. "This is a robbery! All you clerks get your tills open! Anyone tries anything and the whole crowd goes down! Understand?!"

A few people scream and duck under their arms when the gunmen turn their weapons toward the crowd. I stand frozen in shock.

I can't believe this is happening. This is the third disaster in as many days.

All the clerks attack their registers and start opening their cash drawers. The four other gunmen hold the crowd under guard while the first guy grabs a brown paper shopping bag, flicks it open, and goes from register to register.

"Put all the cash in here!" he orders. "Nobody try anything! Everybody keep your hands where I can see them and no one gets hurt!"

The clerks scramble to take out their cash trays and empty them into the bag. I stand stunned and numb while my clerk dumps her cash into the bag and shrinks away.

The guy barges away down the line of registers until he comes to the register in front of the Crenshaws.

The clerk is a young, bony guy barely out of his teens. His hands are shaking so badly that he accidentally drops the cash tray.

It bangs down on the open drawer and a bunch of coins bounce out onto the floor. He fumbles trying to balance the tray and bend over to pick up the coins at the same time.

"Leave it alone, you stupid little shit!" The gunman hauls off and slaps the guy so hard the robber almost knocks the poor kid over. "Dump your cash in here! Don't mess around with that shit!"

"Leave him alone," Ben interjects. "Can't you see he's scared?"

The gunman spins around and aims his weapon straight into Ben's face. "How would you like to be the first to take a mouthful of lead, you stupid piece of shit?"

I cringe. Are we about to watch Ben get shot in some petty grocery store holdup?

Before anyone can move, Ethan flies out of line and tackles the gunman. Ethan reacts so fast that no one sees him coming, especially not the gunman.

Ethan hurls his bulk against the guy and they both topple. They would land flat on the floor, but the gunman clips his head on the counter on his way down.

He falls hard with Ethan on top of him. Ethan doesn't wait a single second before he rears up onto his knees to straddle the guy's chest.

Ethan raises his fist to club the guy, but the gunman lies on the floor with his eyes shut. He's out cold—but not out cold. He isn't breathing.

Ethan freezes there staring down at the gunman's lifeless face. The other robbers move in and hold Ethan at gunpoint, but the robbers can't stop staring at their dead friend.

"He's dead!" one of them husks. "You killed him!"

Ethan raises his dark, haunted eyes to the guy's face. I've never seen Ethan like this before. He always keeps his expression relaxed even when he hangs back and stays silent.

Now he outright glares at the guy in cold-blooded murderous fury. Thank God he isn't looking at me like that.

The gunmen swivel their weapons up to aim at him and he reacts again with impossible speed.

He throws himself sideways onto the floor, rolls, grabs the dead guy's weapon, and tumbles onto his back to aim the gun at the other robbers.

They try to follow his movements, but his sudden maneuver gets the jump on them.

He opens fire and cuts them all down in a split second. None of the other customers or even the Crenshaw boys have a chance to move. It's all over in seconds.

Ethan stays sprawled there on his back aiming the weapon at the empty place where the robbers were just standing. Ethan doesn't move to get up—not until Chuck comes over to him.

"You okay, brother?" Chuck asks.

Ethan has to work hard to tear his eyes away from that spot. He finally nods, but he doesn't relax.

Chuck bends down and squeezes Ethan's shoulder. "Good job, son. Come on. Get up."

He pulls Ethan to his feet. Ethan drops the weapon on the floor and rubs his palm against his pants.

"I'm calling the Police." Chuck pulls out his phone, turns around, and locks his fierce eyes on the clerk. "You okay, buddy?"

The clerk nods fast, but he won't look at anyone.

Chuck glances at Ben. "You okay, son?"

Ben nods, too, but neither he nor Jack speaks. No one in the whole store moves a muscle while Chuck calls the Police and reports everything.

We all stand around in a daze. No one seems to be able to move. I can't even think.

The cops usher everyone out of the building while the Crime Scene people cordon off the store. The five dead robbers are still in there and so are their weapons, including the one Ethan used to kill them all.

The Police go through the whole crowd taking statements from everyone. The cops take Ethan off by himself away from everyone else. I sure hope they don't press charges against him for this.

I hear plenty of people talking about the Crenshaws behind their backs. "He didn't attack until the robbers threatened his brother," one woman remarks.

"Ethan never would stand anyone threatening Ben," a different man adds. "You mess with Ben, you deal with Ethan. It's been like that since they were tiny."

"He didn't mean to kill that first guy," an older woman chimes in. "It was an accident."

My turn comes to give a statement. The officer who takes it is a middle-aged man with greying hair and a thick, greying mustache.

He barely listens when I tell my story. He only nods. "We're getting the same story from everyone."

"Does that mean you're going to let Ethan off?" I ask.

"Probably. Everyone knows the Crenshaw boys. They stick up for each other. It isn't just Ben and Ethan, but they're the touchiest—especially Ethan. You don't mess with the Crenshaws. Pointing a gun at Ben was just stupid—but maybe the idiots were from out of town. It didn't sound from the other statements like they knew who he was—or who any of the boys were."

"I got that impression, too—but I don't know. I'm new in town, too."

He only nods and lets me go. The other customers are already heading for their cars.

I don't want to leave until I know Ethan is going to be okay, but I guess I have no reason to stick around.

The cops finish taking statements from Chuck, Jack, and Ben. The three of them stand over on the other side of the parking lot waiting for the Police to finish questioning Ethan.

The three brothers never take their eyes off the officers involved. I could almost believe the Crenshaws would attack the Police themselves if it meant protecting one of their own.

Chapter 8: Ethan

I walk out of the Police station after giving my second statement to the cops about the grocery store robbery.

I don't regret what I did—not one bit. I would do everything exactly the same way if it happened again.

The cops seem to understand why I reacted the way I did to that guy sticking his gun in Ben's face. All the officers know me. They know how I feel about Ben.

None of that matters because they aren't charging me with a crime. They don't say I'm under investigation or even being considered for criminal charges in the case.

The cops keep telling me that all the witnesses corroborate my story—like I care what they say. No one messes with one of my brothers, especially not Ben.

I swing my truck out of my parking space and take off up the highway. I have a long way to drive back to Turning Point and I've already been gone too long.

Chuck and Wade won't have a problem with me being gone. I'm the one who doesn't like letting the family down when they need me.

I put the grocery store shooting out of my mind and concentrated on the power lines repair. The boys and I still have a week to get the property ready for the repair crew to come out.

That's why we did our monthly shopping trip early. Once the repair crew comes in, no one will be able to get into or out of the driveway for a few days at least. We'll all be stuck there.

I let my thoughts roam over the ranch and all the tasks, jobs, and improvements we still need to do. The lightning storms wreaked havoc in multiple places. We still have to make repairs at Eastwood and Iron Mountain, too.

Almost as if my thoughts make it happen, a fork of lightning sizzles out of the sky right in front of my truck. The strike hits a tree on the mountain nearby.

In seconds, dozens of strikes crackle all over the place. They hit the road, the trees, power poles, and countless other targets.

Torrential wind pounds the side of my truck. I have to fight the wheel to stay on the road, but I'm safe from the lightning as long as I stay inside the vehicle.

I struggle to steer around the next corner. I'm just thinking I should pull over and wait for the storm to pass when I see another car stranded on the shoulder.

The lightning and debris flying back and forth across the windshield makes it difficult to see what kind of car it is.

It sits half-parked in the middle of the lane, but it doesn't flash its hazard lights. I wonder why not.

I pull up alongside, turn on my own hazard lights so cars coming behind me can see me, and I roll my window down.

The other driver rolls down the passenger window—and I look in at Ivy sitting behind the wheel.

She doesn't smile at all this time. She stares at me with huge eyes and then glances at the storm in front of her windshield.

"What happened?" I ask. "Did you break down?"

"I....I don't know....." she stammers and looks down at the dashboard. "I think.....I don't know....I think one of those lightning bolts hit my car. It's an EV. Now it's fried. It won't start—and it doesn't have any other power."

"Come on over," I tell her. "I'll drive you back to town. I'm sure you can get another rental."

She looks up at me, but she barely sees me. She looks terrified.

"Ivy?" I ask. "Are you okay? Come on. Get in the truck. You can't stay out here."

"I....." She glances toward the windshield again. "I don't want to go outside."

"You don't have to. Crawl through the passenger window. You can crawl through my window. I'll move the truck close enough so you don't have to go outside. The cars will protect you."

She looks up at me and her eyes glisten with tears. "Really?"

"Yeah." I lower my voice just a little. "Come on. It will be all right. I'll take you home."

I don't wait for her to respond. I reverse and angle my truck so I'm almost touching her car. I keep my window open and pull up right next to her passenger window.

She's busy gathering up a bunch of files from the passenger seat. She scoots over there and hands me all the files.

I take them from her and put them on top of the dashboard on the passenger side. Then she takes off her shoes, puts them in her briefcase, and hands it to me before she pivots onto her knees on the seat.

She casts one more petrified glance at the lightning dancing all around us. Then she sticks her head and shoulders through the window and starts climbing over me into the truck.

I try to squash myself back against the seat to give her plenty of space. I try to steer her through the tight opening at the same time.

I pretend not to notice her body as she squirms past me. This is an emergency, not a date.

I can't help but catch a whiff of her smell when her body brushes right up against my face. She smells like a combination of peaches and flowers. She smells delicious, but I ignore that.

She finally crawls far enough inside the truck to get her legs over the windowsill. She steps down to balance herself and winds up putting her bare foot on my thigh before she collapses into the passenger seat.

I roll up the window and turn to look at her. I ask, "Are you okay?" before I see her hunched over there fighting back teras.

She compresses her lips, tucks her chin into her chest, and holds her breath so she doesn't break down.

"Hey!" I lean toward her, but I stop myself from touching her. "You're okay! You're safe! Everything is going to be okay."

"I know!" She looks up and winces when she sees the ongoing lightning storm outside. "I was just so scared! I don't know how to thank you!"

"Cut it out," I murmur. "Do you think I would leave you stranded on the side of the road?" I throw caution to the wind, squeeze her shoulder, and wind up rubbing her back. "You're safe now. You're all right. You can relax."

She nods fast, but she won't look up. "I'm sorry. I know I should handle this better."

"You don't have to apologize. Here."

I take a small package of tissues out of my glove box.

I don't keep them around for girls who happen to break down crying in my truck. I keep them for wiping my hands when I need to.

I hand her the package. She takes a tissue out of it and blows her nose.

I sit back in my seat. "Buckle up and I'll drive you home."

She puts the tissue in her lap and I swing the truck around. I set off driving back south toward Coeur d'Alene.

I don't say anything for a while. I'm not sure what to say to her. Getting her home safely is the best thing I can do for her.

I don't like taking even more time away from the ranch, but this is more important. I wouldn't be a Crenshaw if I left some woman in distress.

"I've been meaning to thank you," she croaks. "For what you did at the grocery store. You're a hero."

I look away. "Not really. You could say I have a hair trigger when it comes to my brother—all of my brothers."

She nods. "That's what the other customers said. They said you wouldn't have attacked that guy if he hadn't threatened Ben—but I still want to thank you—on behalf of everyone who was there. You saved us."

I try to shrug it off. "I'm just glad it ended without anyone getting hurt—any of the customers, I mean."

She looks out the window. The lightning seems to be easing off. The wind dies down, so I can drive without worrying about it blowing us off the road.

She finally turns to me. "How are you doing with it all? The Police aren't giving you a hard time about it, are they? I know the other customers all gave statements on your behalf."

"Now, it's all good. I just came from town giving my second statement, but they aren't saying anything about pressing charges. The cops have been really good about it."

"They better be," she mutters.

I glance over, but she's only looking out the window. Maybe that's the end of it.

I'm prepared to drive the rest of the way back to town in silence, but she snaps out of it right away, turns, and smiles at me.

"It was really interesting to visit Gabe in his native habitat. It's nice to see the Crenshaw legacy spreading across the countryside."

I snort. "Maybe it is and maybe it isn't."

"Why wouldn't it be? They seem to be doing well for themselves."

"They have their own problems, especially with all these electrical storms. No one is getting off easy up here."

She inclines her head to study me from the side. "Do you ever think about getting your own place?"

"Nope. I'm perfectly happy at Turning Point. I would do it if the family bought more land and needed me to run it, but I would never leave Turning Point unless I thought it would help out the family."

"What about your other brothers? Do any of them think about going out on their own?"

"I doubt it. Gabe and Jake didn't think about it, either—not until both of those ranches fell into our laps through other circumstances. Gabe and Jake didn't want to leave the ranch."

"Really?" she asks.

I nod, but right then, I turn into the parking lot in front of her duplex. "The lightning is still going on. You should sit tight until it stops."

She turns and smiles up at me—and then that smile starts to fade. She slips her hand across the seat and rests it on top of mine where it rests on my thigh.

"Do you want to come in?" she murmurs.

I stiffen for a second and immediately relax. I don't have to get defensive about this.

"I don't think that's a good idea," I tell her.

"Why? Is it because Ben was flirting with me? Do you guys have some kind of code of honor about not getting involved with someone your brothers are interested in?"

I take a deep breath. "I think you should know that Ben isn't interested in you. He may have been flirting with you, but flirting to him is like racquetball. He does it for fun. It doesn't mean he's serious."

She bursts out laughing. "Yeah! I got that from him."

The warmth of her smile is infectious. I feel myself starting to feel tempted to cave.

I pull it together in time before she rubs her hand across my knuckles. "If he isn't interested, why can't you come inside?"

"It isn't a good idea for me to get involved with you," I tell her again.

"Why not?"

I shrug. "That's just the way it is."

Her face falls. "I don't understand."

"You don't need to. It's my business." I pretend to look outside. "The lightning is easing. You should be able to get inside now."

She stares at me way too intently, and before I can think, she leans in and kisses me.

I find myself responding at first. Her lips feel mind-blowingly soft. They electrify me into responding, but I recover and pull away.

I tell her as gently as I can, "You better go inside."

Her face drains of all color and she looks away. She leans back in her seat, takes her hand away from mine, and looks down into her lap to gather up her stuff.

"I'm sorry if I made you uncomfortable, Ethan," she mumbles. "I'm really grateful to you—for everything."

She scrambles to collect her stuff and puts out her hand to grab the door handle. I see her about to bolt.

I grab her arm above her wrist to hold her back. "You didn't make me uncomfortable. I'm flattered—and you don't have to be grateful to me for anything. Don't worry about it, okay?"

She won't look at me. She just mumbles, "Thank you again," pulls away, and takes off running for her front door. She doesn't even put her shoes on or wait for me to open her door for her.

I shouldn't have let her run out like that. I should have been more polite about turning her down, but I don't see what I could have done differently.

Her door shuts behind her. She isn't here anymore. I have nothing left to do, so I turn around and drive off back home.

Chapter 9: Ivy

I follow the hardware store manage into the warehouse behind the store. This is the first time I've been in here since the truck crash that trapped us inside the building.

He goes around pointing out the fuse boxes, the breaker switches, and some electrical fixtures that need to be upgraded.

I take notes on repairs the company needs to do to bring the building back up to code.

I finish my assessment and head back to my second rental car. This one is not an EV, thank goodness. The insurance company wanted to give me another EV. I refused.

I put my report on the hardware store in my briefcase, take out the files for the grocery store, and turn away to go over there.

The gunmen's bullets tore up the ceiling and shorted out the wiring to the overhead lights and security cameras. The repair crew has to schedule that job on top of everything else.

I make it ten feet from my car before a man comes up to me on the street, seizes my arm in a crushing grip, and yanks me sideways.

I see him steering me toward an alley between the grocery store and the liquor store on the corner.

I yank my arm away from him. "Hey! Leave me alone!"

He gets in my face and hisses at me through his teeth. He's a white guy with sandy, dirty-blonde hair. He's wearing nice casual clothes. He looks clean-cut from the outside.

No one would ever guess he could act so vicious.

"You little bitch!" he snarls. "Did you really think you could get away from me?"

"I don't know what you're talking about! Leave me alone!"

"I will never leave you alone!" he snaps back. "You destroyed my life and I swear I'll make you pay for it. I won't rest until I see you in prison or worse! You may have fooled the rest of the world with your innocent little girl-next-door act, but you don't fool me. I know you're a heartless bitch on the inside. I'll make sure everyone around here knows it, too."

I can't help but bare my teeth at him. "You keep away from me," I growl.

He only leans in closer. "I will never keep away from you—not as long as your bitch ass is walking around free on the street. You screwed me over, but you won't get away with it."

He raises his hand and points in my face. I take a step back and wind up bumping into the wall.

The only other place to go to get away from him is into the alley. It's a blind alley, so if I go in there, I'll be trapped. I can't get away with him standing in front of me.

I might have to fight him off. At least if I start screaming and fighting him someone might intervene.

He doesn't give me a chance. He grabs me by the shoulders, pulls me off the wall, and starts to turn me toward the alley. "Come on," he mutters. "You're coming with me."

I start to struggle again, and right then, Nathan Crenshaw steps between us. He straight-arms the guy away from me and shoves the guy toward the street.

Just as fast, Chuck and Ethan move in to put more distance between me and the guy.

"Back off, pal," Nathan snaps. "I don't think she wants to go anywhere with you."

The guy tries to turn around and fight his way back to me, but he can't go anywhere with the Crenshaws in the way.

Nathan shoves him farther toward the street. "Turn around and walk away, Mister," Nathan barks over the guy's protests. "Pull your head in before you get hurt."

I don't hear what they're talking about, but the guy eventually leaves.

I'm still huddling and shaking against the wall when the three Crenshaws turn around to face me.

"Are you okay?" Ethan asks. "Did he hurt you?"

I shake my head, but I can't look at any of them.

"Did you know that guy?" Chuck casts a flinty glance down the street. "I don't recognize him. He isn't from around here."

"He.......he followed me here....from North Carolina......" I shut my eyes and gulp. "I have a restraining order against him.....That's why I moved here.....to get away from him."

Their features go hard. All three of them narrow their eyes and glare at me, but their presence makes me feel better. I don't have to face this alone.

Ethan holds out his hand, but he doesn't touch me. "You better go to the Police station and report this. Come on. We'll go with you. He won't bother you again."

I stumble down the street in a daze. I wouldn't be able to face any of this without them here.

Ethan stays by my side all the way to the Police station. Nathan tells the officer at the front desk what happened and that I need to file a report—that all four of us need to file reports since the three Crenshaws are witnesses.

The officer tells us to sit down in the waiting area. Ethan sits next to me. Nathan sits on my other side.

Chuck paces around the room like some kind of wild animal in a cage, but it actually feels like a relief that they are all acting so protective.

I cringe in my chair, and pretty soon, a plain-clothes officer comes out of the back and calls me to give my report.

"Do you want me to go with you?" Ethan asks.

"I'll be all right. Thank you for bringing me here."

I go into the back, and when I get out, I find all three of the Crenshaws waiting in the Police station lobby.

"We'll walk you back to your car and follow you home," Ethan tells me. "We'll make sure that guy doesn't come back."

I can only nod. The Crenshaws escort me back to my car.

The workday is already over, so I won't be able to check the grocery store until tomorrow. I couldn't face it right now anyway.

I get into my car, organize my files in my briefcase, and take a deep breath to steady my nerves before I put on my seatbelt and start the motor.

Just then, two trucks pull up on the street nearby. Chuck and Nathan ride in one with Chuck at the wheel. Ethan drives the other truck by himself.

They wait while I reverse out of my space and drive to my place.

The guys get out at the same time I do. They walk me to the door.

Nathan pulls out his phone. "We have your number from the power company paperwork. I'm sending you my number. You call us if you need anything. Understand?"

"I'll send you mine, too," Chuck adds. "Don't hesitate to call."

My phone buzzes in my purse. I can only nod in numb shock. I realize I'm not being as polite or grateful as I should be, but I can't think.

I stumble into my apartment and shut and lock my door behind me. I sink onto the couch in a stupor.

I left North Carolina to get away from a dangerous stalker. Now he's here in Idaho threatening me as much as ever.

Chapter 10: Ethan

I follow Chuck's truck on our way out of Coeur d'Alene. I should be thinking about the ranch and all the work we have to do there.

I can't get Ivy out of my mind—and not because she's beautiful, kind, professional, and obviously attracted to me.

I can't stop thinking about that dirtbag who cornered her on the street. He followed her all the way from North Carolina to Idaho. He doesn't give a shit about any restraining order. He won't give up just because she filed a Police report.

We stop at the last stop light on the way out of town. I give up the war I'm waging against myself, pick up my phone, and call Nathan.

"What's up?" he asks.

"I'm going back. There's something I forgot to do. I'll see you back at the ranch."

"What....Hey!!" He yells out when I flip a U-turn at the light and gun my engines back into town.

I have a bad feeling about leaving Ivy alone. The Police probably won't even take that fool into custody after he violated the restraining order.

I drive back to her duplex, but I park two blocks away where he won't see my truck.

I take my rifle from behind the seat, head into the greenway, come out down the block from her place, and cross the street to the school playground.

I find a place behind the bushes where I can keep her duplex in sight without anyone noticing me.

I don't know how long I'll have to wait for him to show up. I'm prepared to wait all night if necessary.

I spend the time texting my mother and apologizing for the fact that I'll have to miss dinner tonight. I also field a bunch of texts from Wade demanding where I am and what I'm doing.

I repeat that I have something important I need to do in town and that I'll get home as soon as I can.

None of them is satisfied with my non-existent explanation, but that's the best they're going to get out of me right now. I don't even know why I'm here.

I'm just iron-clad certain the guy will come back. He's too determined. He won't just let this slide—whatever it is he has against her.

The sun goes down. It gets dark and the streetlights come on. The neighborhood goes quiet.

The lights switch on in Ivy's duplex. She sits on the couch and works on her laptop.

I probably shouldn't be watching her through her windows without her permission. I shouldn't be watching her at all, but here I am.

I check the time. Eight o'clock turns into nine o'clock and eventually eleven o'clock.

I told myself I would wait all night, but maybe I made a mistake. Maybe I should leave.

I stick around until midnight before the jackass pulls up in his car. The moron parks right in front of her house. He doesn't seem to care about anyone seeing him violate his restraining order—again.

He walks right up to her door and actually tries to open it without knocking. She locked it and he yanks on the knob a few times.

He steps back and kicks in the door. I don't wait around to see anything else.

I march out from behind the bushes, but he's already invading her apartment, grabbing her, and wrestling her down on the floor. She goes down in the living room right where I can see her through the window.

Her screams echo through the front door. That sound does something to me. He is not about to attack her right in front of me. Hell n o.

He flips her onto her stomach and throws a zip tie around her wrists. He bends over her ankles trying to tie them together, too.

She kicks and struggles so much that he doesn't notice me barge through the front door. I could shoot the bastard right here, but I suppose I've shot enough dirtbags for this week.

He looks up and I smash my rifle barrel into his face. He goes down hard, but he doesn't pass out right away. I guess his head is a little harder than most.

He rolls onto his back and looks up at me with his eyes wide open. I don't think so, sonny.

I swing my rifle like a bat and club him across the face. That one really does knock him out.

His head whips sideways and he goes limp on the floor.

I rotate my rifle forward to aim at him just in case he tries anything, but he doesn't move.

I glance over at Ivy and see her gaping up at me in slack-jawed horror. I look away, get busy cutting the zip tie away from her wrists, and pull her onto the couch.

I keep my voice low so she won't think I'm this furious at her. "Sit down here while I call the Police," I tell her.

She follows my directions and sits on the couch in a trance. I hold my phone to my ear and go into the kitchen to get her a glass of water while I wait for the 911 operator to take my call.

I take it back to her and sit next to her while I tell the operator what happened. Ivy drinks the water in a daze.

I finally get off the phone, prop my rifle against the couch, and sit back to wait.

"Are you okay?" I ask her. "I saw everything through the window. Did he hurt you when he took you down?"

She shakes her head and looks down at her hands. "You're always here."

"That asshole was never going to leave you alone. Who is he, anyway? Is he your boyfriend or something?"

"No." She chokes and tears spring to her eyes when she looks around the living room. "He's my brother-in-law—my former brother-in-law--Carl!" She looks down at her hands and tears streak down her cheeks. "You'll think I'm a terrible person. I *am* a terrible person!"

"No, you aren't," I breathe. "He probably wanted you to think that. He wanted to scare you. He wouldn't have followed you here if he didn't want to scare you."

"You don't understand!" she moans. "I killed my husband! His name was Trey and he attacked me. He held a gun to my head and threatened to kill me. He was about to shoot me—and I overreacted. I grabbed a pencil that was lying on the carpet. I didn't even realize what I was doing! I just wanted to get away from him. The pencil went into his neck behind his ear and killed him instantly! The Police let me off, but his brother Carl doesn't believe I did it in self-defense. He came after me to get revenge. That's why I moved here—and now he's here doing the same thing!"

She breaks down crying on the couch next to me.

Every ounce of my being tells me to put my arms around her and comfort her. It takes all my willpower not to.

"Why did you think I would think you were a terrible person because of that?" I ask. "That wasn't your fault. Do you think I'm a terrible person for killing those guys in the grocery store?"

"No!" she wails. "That was different!"

"How was it different? Did you mean to kill your husband?"

"No!" She bursts into racking sobs. "I loved him more than anything!"

I can't stand to see her like this, so I really do put my arms around her. She breaks down completely when I do that, but right then, the cops show up.

I meet them at the door with my hands up. All the same cops from the grocery store lead me outside to take my statement. Then they take Ivy's statement.

They go through a whole lot of back and forth calling the station to check the report my brothers and I gave earlier about this shithead accosting Ivy on the street. The cops they have to search up the restraining order to make sure it's all current and valid.

The cops wind up dragging the guy off in handcuffs even though he's still unconscious.

The cops tell me I have to go back into the Police station to answer more questions later. I agree, but I'm not looking forward to explaining this to my brothers.

I wait for the cops to leave, pick up my rifle, and sit down next to Ivy again. "I better be getting on home. You'll be all right as long as the asshole is in jail."

She looks up at me. She looks unbelievably sad. "Do you have to go? Can't you stay?"

The hair on the back of my neck rises when she says that. I don't have to ask what she means.

I take hold of my rifle. "You can call one of the boys if you need anything."

She lunges for me and grabs my hand. "Don't go, Ethan. Please... .stay...."

This time, I pull my hand out of her grasp. I try to do it gently so she doesn't think I'm recoiling from her.

I have to get away from her right now before this all goes south in a big hurry.

I stand up and head for the door. I say, "Good night," over my shoulder.

"I.....I don't understand....." she falters and gets to her feet, but she doesn't follow me, thank God. "In the truck....you kissed me back......"

I turn around to face her, but even that hurts.

I take a firm grip on myself. I have to end this now. "I have to go," I tell her. "I'm sorry, but nothing can ever happen between us except maybe a one-night stand and I don't do that."

"But....why? Can't you even explain it to me?"

"No, I can't."

I walk out of the house without looking back. I don't let myself hesitate before I walk back to my truck, hang up my rifle, start the motor, and drive off into the night.

Chapter 11: Ivy

I take a deep breath, get out of my car, and face the Iron Mountain ranch house. This is the third property I've assessed that belongs to the Turning Point Ranch Trust.

I have definitely never met anyone like the Crenshaws before. I'm learning that more and more as I continue to deal with them in a professional capacity—and in other capacities.

My respect for them skyrockets off the charts when Jake walks out onto the ranch house porch and hops down the steps to meet me in the driveway.

He limps with one leg in a brace, but he barely notices it. It doesn't slow him down at all, not even when he sticks his bad leg out to the side and hops down the steps on his good leg.

Then he limps with a sideways hitching step and comes toward me smiling with his hand out. "Your reputation precedes you," he tells me when I shake it.

I turn bright red. "It's all exaggerated, I'm sure. I'm really just a pencil-pusher."

He laughs. He resembles Wade and Nathan, but in a much younger, friendlier, almost innocent way.

The rest of his family has already told me chapter and verse about how he got paralyzed in the car accident that killed his father. Now he's married to his former physical therapist, Anna Chamberlain.

She doesn't come out to greet me. The house sounds quiet. Maybe she isn't here.

"So let's get started with this assessment," he tells me. "What do you need to know and what do you need to do?"

"Well, I've been going over the specs on Iron Mountain Ranch to prepare for this meeting and it doesn't look like you suffered any critical damage to your infrastructure during the recent lightning storms. We don't need to do any repairs on your actual property. The major damage is all off the property and already covered under the line repairs the crews will carry out on power company assets—so you don't need to concern yourself with that at all."

He beams at me. "Great. Can I get back to work now?"

I find myself smiling back at him. He's no less steady and determined than the rest of the Crenshaws, but he's much less intimidating.

"Wade and Chuck have approved a major infrastructure upgrade on Turning Point Ranch's power supply. The repair crew is going to do the upgrades at the same time they carry out repairs from the electrical storms."

"What does this have to do with Iron Mountain?"

"The ranch trust's insurance provider is covering the cost of the upgrades—which means we'll be upgrading all three ranches at the same time—Turning Point, Eastwood, and Iron Mountain. The upgrades are already scheduled, so you don't need to do anything about that. I just need to schedule a time for the engineers on the upgrade team to come out here and take a look at everything. They need to assess the infrastructure you already have so they can order parts and outline a plan for the repair crew to carry out the upgrade. I already got Ava to sign off on allowing the engineers access to come on the property and inspect what you already have."

"Then what do you need from me?"

"I just need to know if you have a preferred time or day when you want the team to come. I don't know your schedule or if one day is better than the other."

"Do I need to be here for the assessment?"

"Actually, yes, you do. The engineers also need to assess the house. Access to the house isn't covered under the signed agreement to access the property itself. We need you or Anna to be here to actually grant access in person for the engineers to enter your house."

"Oh, okay. Well, any weekday during business hours should be fine. Just tell me ahead of time which day it is or I might be on the other side of the property and not even realize they're here."

I pull out my day planner. "How about Thursday at ten o'clock in the morning?"

He nods. "Perfect. It's a date."

I laugh and wind up blushing. "You better not let your wife hear you talking like that. Thank you. The engineers will be here then—and I think they'll either call or text you beforehand just to make sure you're here."

"Great. Thank you."

I head for my car. "Thank you. That was easy."

He smiles and waves. "See ya."

I get behind the wheel and reverse out of the driveway. He heads for the barn and doesn't look back at me.

I drive down the driveway and turn out onto the road. I'm just pulling away when three black pickups pull into the driveway at Iron Mountain Ranch behind me.

I don't even have to look to recognize those trucks. They belong to the Crenshaw boys. They must be coming over to help Jake.

They aren't my business anymore. I put them out of my mind and drive down the road on my way back to the highway. I have a long drive back to Coeur d'Alene.

I start thinking of the next property I have to assess. It isn't a Turning Point Ranch Trust property. I've already assessed all three of them. I probably won't have anything to do with the Crenshaws again after this.

That's probably for the best if Ethan is going to be so touchy around me.

I shouldn't even be thinking about him, but I can't help it. He staked out my duplex because he thought Carl would come after me.

Ethan must have been thinking about me. He went out of his way to protect me.

Every other time, he was either with his brothers or out in public somewhere. He wasn't that time.

He helped me when my car broke down, too, but he said he would do that for anyone. It wasn't personal.

Him waiting outside my duplex and intervening when Carl attacked—that was personal. How long did Ethan have to wait outside before the jackass showed up?

Ethan is such a strong, admirable man. Everyone looks up to him. His brothers obviously think the world of him.

Anyone can see he has his issues, though. He already told me nothing can happen between us.

I just need to distance myself from him. I need to put him as far out of my mind as possible and move on. He's too messed up for me to hang around waiting for him to come to his senses.

I can't even blame his upbringing for this. Ben doesn't have any problem talking to women. His family seemed to think he didn't have a problem getting involved with them, either.

Ethan has his own demons to fight. He obviously wants to fight them alone without any help from me or anyone else.

I have my own problems. I don't need to go around solving someone else's.

I need to follow up with the Police to find out what's going on with Carl. I don't even know what they're doing about him breaking into my apartment.

The instant I think that, a different pickup swoops up behind me. I was so lost in my thoughts that I didn't notice it before.

This is a different make of truck than the Crenshaws drive. It can't be one of them.

The truck roars alongside my car like the driver wants to pass me. I instinctively slow down to let the person speed ahead.

Instead, the truck swerves hard and smashes into me from the side. I scream out and fight the wheel to hold the car on the road.

The truck overpowers my flimsy rental car in seconds. Heavy tinting blocks out the truck's side windows. I can't see who the driver is, but only one person alive wants to kill me this badly.

Is it possible the Police just let Carl go after he attacked me in my apartment? Did he already get out of jail and now he's coming after me again?

The truck revs its engines to a shriek and yanks harder into my lane. I can't hold the wheel steady. The truck starts to force me onto the shoulder.

I scream again when I see a guard rail cutting across the side of the road. A steep gulley plunges down beyond the hill into a wooded ravine.

I can't even scream anymore. I see my car driving straight for the guard rail. I can't stop it.

I hit the brakes to try one last hopeless time to break away from the truck, but the mystery driver reacts too fast, dives the rest of the way into my lane, and plows me straight off the shoulder into the trees.

My car doesn't even make it as far as the guard rail before the shoulder plunges downward into the woods beyond.

Holding onto the steering wheel doesn't help me at all now. I throw my arms over my face as tree branches smash in the windshield and slam all over the roof and sides.

The car nose-dives down, down, down into a black ravine. The car bumps over things, bounces off of things, and then hits an obstacle and launches off the ground.

The car plummets through more thick branches, breaks clear, dives down to plunge below the canopy, and smashes nose first into the opposite side of the ravine walls.

The car creaks, slams back onto its wheels, and comes to rest with its nose pointed uphill. Too many trees block the car from rolling the rest of the way down the ravine.

I peer through the broken driver's window. The car lands fifteen feet from the gulley floor. A tiny stream winds through the very bottom.

Towering forests and steep mountains surround me on all sides. No one can see my car from the road. No one knows where I am.

I pull out my phone, but my hands are shaking too badly. I have trouble unlocking the screen. I need to call the Police—but how can I report this? No one saw the truck drive me off the road.

I didn't see the driver, either. I can't say for certain that it was Carl. No one else will be able to identify him, either. No one else was there.

I tap on the phone icon, but I get an error message. My phone shows zero bars of reception. I'm stranded in the middle of the remote Idaho woods with no way to call for help.

I take a few deep, steadying breaths. I'll just have to walk out of here. That could take a while considering where I am—and I don't even know which direction to walk.

I'm wearing my heels for work today, but I do have a pair of workout sneakers in the back of my car. I'll be able to walk a long way in them.

I try to use my phone to find out both where I am and which is the best route back to the road, but I can't connect to the internet, either. I'll just have to do this the old-fashioned way.

I push my door open. It creaks and gets stuck halfway. The hinge must have gotten bent when the car hit all those trees.

I have to use my foot to force the door the rest of the way open.

I kick off my heels on the floor in front of the driver's seat. This car is another rental. At least I don't have to worry about replacing this car, too.

I step out onto a spongy bed of fallen pine needles. They prick my bare feet, but not for long. I just have to get my sneakers out of the trunk.

I take one step and freeze when a twig snaps somewhere above me. I hold my breath to listen—and realize it isn't a twig.

Something is coming down the hill crashing through the branches. Whatever it is doesn't even try to be quiet. It's a person.

I charge back to the driver's seat, dive for my purse, and scramble to pull out the semi-automatic pistol I take with me everywhere.

This is the reason I moved to Idaho in the first place and not some other Western state. The gun laws here are much less restrictive. I don't need a license to carry a weapon.

I could carry it on my person, but I still haven't figured out how to do that during work hours when I'm wearing a business suit.

Carl surprised me in my apartment that night. He caught me and tackled me before I could get to my gun.

I started looking at holsters and other ways to carry the gun on my person since his last attack, but I haven't decided yet which holster I want or which carry would be best for my work attire.

That doesn't matter because I grab the gun out of my purse just as he breaks through the undergrowth.

The bruises from Ethan knocking him out still discolor Carl's face, but he still looks mad as hell. He's much madder now than he was when he confronted me on the street.

He storms down the hill toward me and compresses his lips in fury. I shrink back from him, but I only wind up bumping into the car.

My heart stops when I realize I can't get away from him. He's coming too fast. I would have to run past him to go anywhere.

I aim my gun at him, but my hands are shaking too badly for me to aim very well.

"Stop!!" I choke.

He doesn't stop. He curls his lip back from his teeth, sticks his hand behind him, and pulls out his own gun.

Time slows as he sweeps his arm around his body. He rotates his elbow to bring the gun up to point it at me. I can't let him do that.

Carl and my late husband Trey both knew how to use guns. Carl can aim so much better than I can. I have to stop him before he gets to me—and before he fires his weapon at me.

I pull the trigger, but I can't even think clearly enough to aim.

The gun explodes in my hands. The noise deafens me and I scream out more from terror that I'm actually shooting at someone.

His head whips back and he topples flat on his back on the ground. I stare in utter horror when I see part of his head, eye, and face missing. I actually hit him. He's lying dead on the ground in front of me.

I scream again and take off running. I'm too hysterical even to see or think about where I'm going. I only know I have to get away from all of this before the whole world falls apart around my ears.

Chapter 12: Ethan

I get out of my truck and meet up with Jake outside the corral at Iron Mountain ranch.

Chuck gets out of his truck and Jack and Nathan get out of Nathan's truck.

"Was that Ivy Harper I just saw pulling out?" Nathan asks. "Didn't she already do an assessment on Iron Mountain?"

"She didn't come to do an assessment," Jake tells us. "The ranch doesn't need repairs done on the property. All the damage is off the property in the power company's regular network. The repair crews are already covering that."

"What was she doing here, then?" Jack asks. "Don't tell me she's got a thing for married men now."

Jake laughs. "I wouldn't know anything about that. She came because the engineers need to check the infrastructure to do the upgrades you boys are scheduling. The engineers need to come and see what we already have—and they need to go into the house and check that, too. It's all covered under the insurance policy, so they just need to take a look and I need to be here to let them into the house. She just wanted to schedule the time and make sure I'm going to be here."

Chuck squints up the hill. A bunch of wild horses canter around in the pasture up there. They sure look happy.

A kind of blessed light shines over Iron Mountain Ranch. I never spent much time here before Jake and Anna took over this place.

It sure looks nice now. It looks like a slice of Heaven where good horses go when they die. I can't remember seeing happier, more relaxed horses anywhere, not even at Turning Point.

"So what do you need us to do?" Chuck asks. "Nathan says you need to fix something or other, but Hank seems to think you don't need our help at all—so which is it?"

Jake laughs, but right then, we hear a gunshot not far away followed by a woman screaming. It sounds way too close.

We all stiffen at the sound. Chuck cocks his head to one side. "Did that come from your property?"

"It sounded like it came from the gulley down the back," I point out. "Let's go check it out, boys."

We split up to our trucks. Chuck, Nathan, and I grab our rifles from the racks behind the seats. Nathan pulls a shotgun from under his seat and hands it to Jack.

Jake takes off hobbling extra fast toward his house, springs up the steps amazingly fast considering he has a disabled leg, and grabs his rifle from right inside the door.

He comes back to join us on our way down the driveway. We turn off onto a side path cutting alongside one of his pastures.

Jake has no problem keeping up with us even when the path plunges down the gulley into the woods behind the property.

We spread out. Jake stays on the path where he can walk more easily. Chuck, Nathan, Jack, and I separate and advance more slowly through the trees.

We don't hear anything at first. We inch our way down the hill into the ravine.

I keep my rifle jammed into my shoulder, but I aim at the ground even though there's nothing out here.

The boys and I pass our rifles back and forth around the area searching for anything out of the ordinary. The canopy gets thicker and casts the forest floor in shadow. It makes the whole area look spooky and menacing.

Goosebumps break out all over my body. Something is out here. I know it is.

We hear footsteps coming up the hill long before we see anyone—and we hear someone gasping, panting, and sobbing in misery.

All five of us turn our guns in that direction as the sound gets louder and closer.

My world stops when Ivy staggers out of the trees barefoot and bawling her eyes out. She bursts into loud, painful sobs when she sees us and stumbles faster up the hill.

She's holding a gun in one hand. She points it at us when she extends her arms toward us—and then waves it behind her at the shadows down the hill.

I raise my rifle to aim back at her before I realize she's too distraught to know what she's doing.

She doesn't notice when the other boys stop in their tracks holding her at gunpoint. I keep advancing toward her. Something is wrong—seriously wrong. I've never seen her this upset—not even when her former brother-in-law broke into her house and tried to kidnap her.

She howls with broken sobs, turns in my direction, and staggers straight into my arms. Her legs give out before she gets to me. She collapses against me wailing and shrieking in wordless, incoherent sobs.

"What happened?!" I have to yell to make myself heard over her noise. "What happened?! What are you doing down here?!"

She only sobs louder if that's possible. She waves her gun down the hill again.

I glance in that direction. I don't see anything but dim shadows down there.

Chuck saves the day by striding past us on his way down the hill. Jack and Nathan go with him. Jake stands guard over me while I pull Ivy to her feet.

"Come on!" I tell her. "We'll take you back to the house."

She won't stop howling. She holds onto me in a death grip and doesn't let go when I make her stand up.

I want to know what's down there and what she's doing out here waving a gun around, but she's more important.

I turn around and start climbing the hill. She stumbles on her bare feet. She can hardly hold herself up.

Jake comes with me and keeps his rifle ready. He keeps casting glances all around us in case anything or anyone comes.

We make it back to the path before Chuck and the others catch up with us.

"That son of a bitch is down there with his head shot off," Chuck mutters and pulls out his phone.

He holds it to his ear and starts barking into the phone on our way back to the house. "This is Chuck Keller calling from Iron Mountain Ranch." He gives the emergency operator the address. "There's a dead man out here with a gunshot wound to his head, a gun in his hand, and a woman who is hysterical out of her mind and raving while she waves a gun around. Her car is crashed at the bottom of the ravine with scratches and body damage on one side. It looks like someone ran her off the road and then tried to kill her. Yes, Ma'am, we have the woman at the ranch house. You can find us here."

He hangs up and gives Ivy a deadly look before he looks away. I know exactly how he feels.

Ivy won't let go of me to save her life. We get back to the house just as Anna is getting out of her car.

She stares at us and then rushes in to take care of Ivy. Ivy is still too worked up to say a word to any of us when Anna takes her inside. We can all hear Anna talking and Ivy wailing and sobbing through the open house door.

"Holy flippin' shit," Jack mutters. "Can we all just forget about this asshole now?"

"He's dead, son," Chuck tells him. "No one ever has to deal with the cocksucker again."

"Except for her," Jake points out. "Now she has to live with the reality that she killed him. A woman doesn't get over that anytime soon."

That kills the conversation. I have a hard enough time standing on the porch listening to her crying in there.

It's a damn good thing her brother-in-law is dead. I have a mind to march down the ravine right now and kill the bastard a second time for doing this.

The five of us stand around waiting until the cops show up. They bring the whole Crime Scene unit with them.

Detective Rod Newcastle comes with them. He gives me a hard look when he sees me standing there with my brothers. "Tell me you didn't have something to do with this again," he mutters.

"No, Sir," I tell him. "I never even saw the son of a bitch."

"None of us saw him until he was already dead," Chuck interrupts. "We found her stumbling through the woods half out of her mind.

Then the three of us went down there and found her car crashed and him already dead. He's still down there if you want us to show you where."

Rod surveys all five of us. "Jake, you better be the one to show us. You boys stay here until I get back."

"Yes, Sir," Jake replies and hops down the steps.

He leaves with Rod and the Crime Scene people. They don't come back for a long time.

"It's just as well you weren't there," Chuck mumbles while we wait. "You're gonna have a rap sheet for the record books the way you're going."

I look away. I wish I had been there. I wish I had been the one to shoot that piece of shit instead of her.

When they do come back, Rod and Jake come alone. Rod questions all of us one after the other, but of course none of us can tell him anything. I can tell him the least of everyone.

He tells us we can go and then he goes inside to talk to Ivy. I really wish I could go in there and be there for her when she tries to explain this to the Police.

I can't do that and there is no way on God's green Earth I would ever ask her what happened—not again.

I already know what happened. I don't need the details.

Chuck bumps Nathan in the shoulder. "Let's get out of here. Whatever you need doing around here can wait, Jake."

"Yes, Sir," Jake replies. "The mobile network is back up and running. You can call me when you're ready to come back over."

Chuck levels me with an appraising glance. He knows me too well not to read exactly what I'm thinking. "You coming?"

I look past him toward the trucks. "You go on. I'll catch up with you."

He only nods before he, Jack, and Nathan leave.

Jake goes inside and leaves me standing alone on the porch, thank the stars. They all know better than to ask me anything.

Chapter 13: Ivy

I can't stop bawling my eyes out or look at anyone. I can't believe it. I shot Carl.

Killing Trey was bad enough. I never resented Carl for hating me for that.

Now Carl is dead, too. I didn't mean to kill him. I didn't even think I was aiming at him.

I can't get the picture out of my head of his skull blasted off and him lying there with his one eye still staring up at the sky.

Now the gun lies on the living room coffee table at Iron Mountain Ranch. The gun stares back at me accusing me of killing Carl.

Anna sits next to me with her arm around my shoulders, but her attention and support only make me feel worse.

I'll never be as good as the Crenshaws. They're all so much better than I can ever hope to be.

Anna keeps rubbing my back and hugging me. She doesn't know I'm bad luck.

Death follows me everywhere. I can't even move across the country without it tracking me down.

I wasn't trying to kill Trey or Carl. I never wanted to kill anyone.

A different man walks into the house. He wears a blue business jacket over a black shirt and clean blue jeans. He also wears cowboy boots and a large black cowboy hat.

I barely glance at him and look away when I see a gold badge hanging from his belt. He wears a sidearm in a holster on his other hip.

He sits down in the armchair across from us. "Hello, Ivy. I'm Detective Rod Newcastle of the Coeur d'Alene Police Department. Can you tell me what happened?"

I break down crying my eyes out. How in God's name am I supposed to explain any of this?

I open my mouth more than once, but no sound comes out. He waits. He acts like he can wait all day.

"Let's go back in time," he finally suggests. "What brought you out here to Iron Mountain today? Why are you so far out of town."

"She had to do an assessment on the ranch for the power company," Anna interjects. "She came to see about repairing the damage."

"Is that right, Ivy?" he asks. "Is that why you came out here?"

I nod down at my hands.

"I wasn't here," Anna goes on. "She was talking to Jake."

Just then, Jake walks into the room. Detective Newcastle looks up. "So Ivy came out here to talk to you about the repairs?"

"Yes, Sir," Jake replies. "We talked and then she got in her car and left. Then the boys showed up and we were talking when we heard the gunshot and the scream."

Detective Newcastle turns back to me. "So you left the ranch after you finished your conversation. Then what happened? Did you plan to drive back to Coeur d'Alene?"

I open my mouth again, but it takes me an almighty effort to make a sound. "I.....I had to....check another property....." I start crying again for no apparent reason. "At Hollow River Hill....."

I wave behind me. No one says anything. The silence becomes oppressive.

The gun on the table looks so damning. It bears silent testimony to what a bad person I am. I killed two men. I'm worse than the Black Plague.

Detective Newcastle reads my mind, pulls a large ziplock bag out of his inner jacket pocket, turns it inside out, and uses the bag's inner surface to pick up the gun.

He flips the bag right-side out and the gun falls into the bag without him touching it. He seals the bag, walks out of the house, and comes back without the gun before he resumes his seat.

"Now let's get back to what happened when you left Iron Mountain," he goes on as if none of that business with the gun ever happened. "Chuck thinks someone ran into your car—and he's right. The scratches and body damage on the righthand side seem to indicate that someone ran you off the road. Is that right?"

I nod fast. I can't do this anymore. I need to get this over with and get out of here. I can't stand this.

"It was a black.....black pickup truck....." I blurt out. "With black ....tinted windows.....I didn't see the driver.....He ran into me....on the road out there...."

I wave toward the driveway, but I can't be sure anymore if I was driving in that direction when it happened.

Detective Newcastle frowns, pulls out his phone, and makes a call. "Search the roads around Iron Mountain Ranch. See if you can find a black pickup with dark tinted windows and any kind of body damage on the left side. It should be over near the Rootless Gulley crossing."

He hangs up and turns back to me. "If your former brother-in-law did drive you off the road and then come after you with a gun, his truck should be parked near the top of the gulley where he could follow you down there."

I nod fast. "I heard him......I heard him coming.....when I got out of the car.....he came after me......"

"Did he shoot at you first before you shot him?"

I cast my eyes down at my hands in my lap, but I can't see them through my tears. "He didn't shoot. He didn't even point the gun at me. He was taking it out and starting to raise it." I break down sobbing again. "I didn't mean to kill him! I just wanted to stop him from shooting at me! It was the same thing with Trey! I didn't want anyone pointing a gun at me anymore! I didn't think I was aiming well enough to hit him! I don't even know how to aim a gun!"

Detective Newcastle looks up at Jake and nods. Jake moves forward. "Come with me, Ivy," he murmurs. "Ethan is waiting to take you home."

I can't see straight enough to get out of the house. Jake has to steer me by the elbow.

I don't let myself think about what it means that Ethan is waiting to drive me home. I don't care. I hate myself for even being in the same room with these wonderful people.

Jake pushes open the front door. Ethan stands there alone leaning against one of the porch support posts.

He stands up straight and turns toward me when Jake brings me out. None of them says a word when Ethan takes over, escorts me down the steps, and opens the passenger door of his truck.

All my paperwork, my phone, my purse, my shoes, and everything else is still down there at the bottom of the gulley. I don't dare to go down there to get any of it.

Don't ask me how I'm going to explain it to my boss that I left power company case files in an abandoned car at the bottom of a ravine.

The Crime Scene people might take all of that into evidence. That would be just great.

I'm crying too hard to do anything about that now. Ethan gets behind the wheel, pulls out of the driveway, and starts on the long, silent drive back to Coeur d'Alene.

I can't even regret that he was the one who grabbed me when I first stumbled upon him and the Crenshaw boys in the gulley. I couldn't think of anything except getting somewhere safe—somewhere Carl couldn't get to me.

No one is safer than Ethan. He's always there when I need him and he always protects me. I'm sure any of the others would have done the same thing, but he's different. I feel differently about him.

Neither of us says a word all the way back to Coeur d'Alene. I don't know what to say except to maybe apologize to him for making myself an inconvenience to him again.

He didn't have to stay behind and drive me home after his brothers left. Does it mean anything that he did?

He parks in front of my duplex and turns off the motor. I understand the Crenshaws well enough by now. I'm supposed to sit here and wait for him to get out and open my door for me.

He doesn't get out. He sits in the driver's seat and stares through the windshield at my building.

He can see through the front window to the living room beyond. He saw everything that happened the night Carl broke in.

Does Ethan even suspect how much I really don't want to go into my apartment alone? Does he even know how hard that will be after everything that happened today?

I can't ask him to come in—not again—and I don't. My self-respect might be in the toilet right now, but I can't fall as far as that.

I'm just about to thank him for driving me. Maybe then he'll get the message to let me out and he'll leave. I'll bite the bullet and face going home alone.

He turns to look over at me. His dark eyes connect with mine and he extends his arm over the back of my seat.

"Come here," he murmurs and pulls me against him.

I collapse against his chest and his arms fold around me. That feeling of him holding me breaks down the last barrier.

I start sobbing even harder, now that he's finally holding me. He held me all the way out of that ravine. He held me all the way back to Jake's house.

This is different. I can actually break down in misery that my life is such a wreck. He doesn't care. He just holds me while I let it all out.

Holding onto him feelings so incredibly good. There's no judgment in anything he does. He doesn't think I'm a terrible person because I killed two men.

What in the world am I thinking? He killed five men in the grocery store and I think he's one of the best men I've ever met.

He could have killed Carl the other night. I wouldn't have thought any worse of Ethan if he did kill Carl.

Thank the stars in Heaven Ethan was there when I came out of the ravine. I couldn't have coped if it had been anyone else—and now he's here.

He must have realized he was the only person who could bring me home. He's the only person I can think of who makes this better.

Everything is better because of him. I can live with it as long as he's here—because he just accepts it. He thinks nothing of me killing two men in self-defense.

I shouldn't think anything of it, either. That's what his arms tell me when he holds me like this.

He grips the back of my head and presses me tighter into his shoulder while I cry. He wants me here.

I already know he won't take it any further. He won't let it turn into anything more. He already said so and I respect him too much to push something he doesn't want.

I pull away from him. His hands slide around my waist when he lets me sit up.

Tears pour down my cheeks. I don't even care that he's seeing me so messed up. He's the only person who can see me like this—because he understands. He understands why I need to fall apart over this.

I should go inside. I'm just about to tell him so and thank him again when he raises his hand and passes his warm fingers across my cheeks to wipe my tears away.

His eyes soften in ways they never have before. He gazes down deep into my eyes. There's no question in my mind. He's looking at me like that. He feels something for me—something of what I feel for him.

He keeps caressing his fingers and thumbs over my cheeks to wipe my tears away—and then he passes his thumb across my lips.

His eyes dart down to my mouth—and he kisses me.

His hands close on either side of my face to pull me into his lips. His mouth softens in ways it didn't that time when I kissed him. He responded then, but only barely.

He does more than respond now. He escalates faster than I ever expected.

He kisses me deeper and his tongue laces into my mouth—just once—just enough to shoot a blistering jet of fire into my deepest being.

He kisses me like that once and pulls away to gaze down at me again. He doesn't look away.

His expression churns with so many shades of emotions, but I don't see any doubt in there—not about kissing me.

Why is he kissing me when he said he doesn't want anything serious with me?

Chapter 14: Ivy

I force myself to look away from Ethan. I would almost rather go inside my apartment by myself and face this waste of a life of mine than for him to kiss me for no reason.

"I should go," I husk.

He gets out, walks around the truck, and opens my door. I can't look at him when he walks me to the door.

He stops there while I get the spare key out of the potted plant. I left my regular keys in the car.

I'll have to find a new hiding place for the spare key now, but I don't even care about that.

I unlock the door and turn back to Ethan. There's nothing left to do but for me to go inside and for him to drive back to Turning Point where he belongs.

I don't even want him here if he doesn't want anything from me. I would rather just forget I was ever attracted to him.

I don't even get a chance to thank him before he takes my hand, leads me into the apartment, and shuts the door behind him with a final, ominous click. What is he doing in here?

He doesn't leave me in any doubt. He takes a step toward me, takes the key out of my hand, wraps his arms around my waist, and picks me up off the floor kissing me for all eternity.

That kiss blasts me full of heat and passion. His tongue feels incredible in my mouth. His muscular body doesn't hold back from me one bit.

He kisses me madly, ravenously. He attacks my mouth like he's been holding himself under a tight leash all this time.

All this crying and fear these last few days—they leave me ragged and clingy. I need him. I need him to be here with me just like this—and now he is.

I don't know what this means. It might only be for one night, but I need him more than anything. I can't face tonight without him.

I kiss him back trying in every possible way to keep up with him. He can't touch me when he's holding me up like this—and then, without warning, he dives one hand down to my ass.

He clamps me between my legs from behind and holds me up like that, but my tight business skirt won't let him get any deeper between my legs.

The extra pressure between my legs explodes me out of my mind. Insatiable desire breaks through me and aching hunger burns me between my legs. I need him. I need him to take me right now.

He doesn't back down—not once. He keeps kissing me—and then he pulls me harder against him so I feel his bulging package digging between my thighs. He wants it. He wants it bad—and he wants it n ow.

His lips snatch my breath away. My eyes float open and I see him staring at me out of the dark depths of his soul.

He keeps his eyes open while he devours my mouth. He would have to be dead not to feel how much he makes me vibrate for him.

I want to wrap my body around him right now and feel every inch of him taking me.

He reads my mind, carries me into my living room, sits down on the couch, and pulls me sideways to sit on his lap.

He immediately starts kissing me just as passionately. He doesn't try to stop me from sitting on his hard knob right under my ass.

I moan and sigh when I twist my ass on top of it. I don't care if he knows how much I want him.

He cradles the back of my neck with one hand to hold me up. He rests his other hand on my hip and winds up guiding my ass in gyrating circles on his lap.

His arms steer me where he wants me to go in an unmistakable sexual rhythm.

I get lost in the magic of that kiss. I can forget everything in the bliss of him holding me, touching me, and pulling me into him.

I don't know if it will ever go any further than this. I don't need for it to go any further than this.

I just need to feel that he wants me and for him to feel that I want him. I need to know he isn't rejecting me for some bizarre reason he won't even explain to me.

I sensed in the truck that time that he wanted to keep going. He has his own reasons not to and that's okay.

I'm not here to make it go further. I'm just riding this wave of rapturous pleasure for as long as it lasts.

I feel safe with him. I feel safer with him than I ever felt with my late husband. I've never felt this safe with anyone.

I don't want to lose this beautiful safety. Even if it never goes any further, I want to stay here as long as I can.

All thought that it won't go further evaporates out of my mind when he slides his hand up under my skirt. He squeezes my thigh in one crushing grip—and his fingers find my saturated panties.

He rubs in tiny circles over my mound until I whine and moan with unstoppable pleasure. I want him so bad.

He slips his fingers into my panties and I scream into his mouth when his fingers drill inside me.

I thrash and toss on his fingers when he drills me all the way in. I can't stop moaning and roaring in his mouth as his fingers drive me over the edge.

I buck hard against his hand as a mind-blowing orgasm cascades through me to the ends of time.

He only holds me tighter and kisses me deeper as the storm breaks. He doesn't let me go as all this ragged emotion comes breaking to the surface.

He doesn't pull out until I start to cycle down. I drift back to consciousness to find his eyes hovering in front of me.

They still look soft, but some of the hard, flinty intensity I know so well creeps back into his gaze.

I sink into his arms in a daze, but he won't stop kissing me. He never lets me rest.

He puts his hand on my hip again—on the outside of my skirt. I prepare myself to wind back down and maybe even thank him and say good night.

Nothing prepares me for the moment when he slides his hand up to my waist, squeezes, and then inches higher to my ribs. He squeezes me once right below my breast—just enough to warn me of what he's going to do.

My breath catches—and then his hand closes on my breast in a hard, comforting grip.

He massages in deep, warm circles for a second—just enough to escalate my desire for him back to the pitch of fevered excitement it was before.

His package pulsates under my ass. He keeps digging it into me every time I convulse on his lap. He doesn't try to make it less obvious what he wants to do with that hard spike.

He pulls off my mouth and his eyes hold me captive while he tugs off my blazer.

His eyes go hard again when he starts unbuttoning my blouse. He holds me spellbound with that unwavering stare. He's doing this. He's taking my clothes off. He wants to go all the way.

I tremble before the power of that stare. He sees how much he turns me on. I don't try to hide it, either, but he's the first man who ever really saw it. No one else ever even looked for it—not like this.

He pulls my blouse out of my waistband and tugs that off my shoulders, too. He lays it on the couch behind me so I sit in front of him in my bra.

He settles back on the couch to admire me in my bra. No man has ever done this before, either.

He traces his fingertips down my cleavage, touches the lace edging, and back up the straps to my shoulders. He caresses across my bare chest and collarbones and up my neck.

That feather makes me shiver and gasp. He watches my lips tremble and my eyes drift out of focus when he drags his knuckles extra lightly over my bra cups to tease my nipples.

He glides up my straps to my shoulders again.....and eases them off extra slowly. I shrug out of them and he unclips my bra behind my back.

He doesn't have to look. Has he done this before? He sure acts like it. He acts like he does it all the time.

He pulls my bra away extra slowly, but he doesn't look at my bare breasts. He stares unbelievably deep into my eyes. He pays more attention to my facial expressions and reactions than to my breasts themselves.

He pulls me in and starts kissing me again. That kiss rises to the same fevered tempest of barely contained passion.

His big, strong hand closes on my bare breast, and this time, he starts playing with my nipples.

He squeezes and then pinches them between the flat edges of his fingers. He does it to both of my breasts until I whine and cry out in his mouth as my desire spikes off the charts.

I can't stop grinding on his lap. He turns me on so much I can't stand it.

I can't stand it if he ends this without taking me. I need him—all of him.

He tears off my mouth with a feral growl and dives into my chest. He closes his hand on my breast to steer it into his mouth.

I scream when he inhales my nipple and starts sucking for all he's worth. He lets go with his hand and plunges under my skirt again.

I crash into another devastating orgasm when he drills his fingers in hard, mauls my nipples one after the other in brutal, animal hunger, and thrusts his fingers in to drive me to my limit.

I'm still screaming out of my mind when he lowers my head and shoulders onto the couch, pushes my skirt up, and crawls down between my legs.

He pulls my panties aside and I scream again in torrential madness when his mouth takes hold of my tender flesh.

His lips and tongue light me on fire. He pulls my thighs around his head and throws his hat off when he starts mauling me in big, wolfish mouthfuls.

He wears his hair buzzed extra short. It gives him an even harder, more immovable look. He's so different from Ben, but Ethan is so much more attractive precisely because he's more serious and intense.

He keeps grabbing handfuls of my ass and thighs while he consumes me out of my mind—and then his fingers find their way back inside me.

I rear off the couch driving myself against his face. I can't get enough of him. I rub his head and try to pull him in tighter, but he takes his time and eats me out at his own pace.

He uses my movements to lift my flesh into his mouth. He keeps pushing my thighs apart, gripping his fingers deep into my ass, and hooking his hand under my knee to push my legs farther up so he can devour me.

Chapter 15: Ivy

I can't stop thrashing on the couch climaxing again and again. Ethan doesn't stop devouring me between my legs—until he does stop.

I wilt whining and moaning on the couch as he crawls up my body and lays all his weight on top of me.

He rotates his hips between my thighs, but he's still fully dressed except for his hat.

He kisses me beyond deep. His lips and tongue taste like my juices. He rocks his hips into me and drills the hard knob of his jeans into my sensitive clitoris.

I scream again, but his kisses silence me. His body strains with muscle under his shirt.

I can't stand this. I need him more than anything. I can't lie here and take this without feeling him inside me.

I open my eyes just as he opens his. He breaks off my mouth and pushes himself up on his arms to look down at me with eagle eyes.

I sway under him half naked. He sees me totally exposed.

I hold his gaze as I move my hands to his belt buckle. I want to touch him. I want to feel his hardness.

I don't even know if he'll let me do that, but I have to try.

He doesn't stop me when I pull his belt loose. I tug his shirt out of his jeans, but his vest gets in the way of me taking his shirt off.

He stays there on his arms while I tug his vest off the way he tugged my jacket off.

He shifts his weight from one arm to the other to shrug out of his vest.

Now it's my turn to hold eye contact while I unbutton each and every button of his shirt. I want to see what he looks like under his clothes. I want to see how big and muscular he is.

My desire for him rises to insanity when I push his shirt open and my hands stroke up his bare chest. His body tenses at my touch. His eyes clamp shut once and he plunges in to kiss me.

I can't get enough of touching him. I caress his chest, down to his stomach, and then up his bare back under his shirt while he buries me under his weight.

He closes his arms around me pumping between my thighs. He holds me in a death grip as his heat sears down on my bare breasts and stomach.

I try again and again to get his shirt off, but he's holding onto me too tightly. It takes him a long time before he eases off enough to pull his arms out of the sleeves.

He props himself up on his arms and fixes his hawkish gaze on me again when I trail my fingertips back down his stomach to his waistband.

His powerful chest, shoulders, and back swell above me in a wall of dark muscle. This is it. I'm about to unzip him and then nothing will separate him from me.

I unbutton his jeans. He's so throbbing hard that his zipper practically falls open by itself when I slide it down over his bulging package.

He gasps once through his nose when I dive my hand inside his shorts and take hold of him. He shuts his eyes only for a moment and then glares at me when I start stroking him.

His eyes go hard as dark chips of fire as his body tenses. His thick shaft swells in my hand. The heat radiating off him blisters my skin. I don't know if I can cope with the intensity of what I'm about to do.

He doesn't kiss me to make it easier. He watches my eyes floating in a haze of sex and we haven't even done it yet.

He lets me push his jeans and shorts down. He doesn't look away even for a second when he kicks them off along with his boots.

I hold onto his iron rod until he's ready. I just don't know if I'm ready. He locks on my eyes through it all. He doesn't move in. He waits for me to make the first move to cross that line.

He feels too thick and strong and hot not to take him—in there where I really need him.

I guide him deeper between my legs, rub his thick, swollen head through my dripping tissues, and arch my hips up to take him inside.

He waits until right that moment to sink into me—just enough to break the barrier between us.

I gasp as he splits me open. He doesn't lower his weight on top of me again. He stays up there like a god on his arms where he can watch me panting, whining, and grimacing as he corkscrews all the way inside.

He flexes his hips in an excruciating spiral drilling movement to plunge all the way to my depths. I can't look away from his intoxicating eyes.

He plows in deep, screws me in circles to fill me to the breaking point, and arches out just as slowly.

I scream when I feel every powerful inch of him excite me to the stratosphere—and then he does it all over again when he pulls out for the next thrust.

I claw at him, grab his arms and shoulders, grip his ass to pull him in faster and harder—I do a thousand things trying to take all of him at once.

He holds his own rhythm here, too. He never goes any faster until he decides to do it.

He picks up the pace, but he does it slowly. He stays up there above me where he can see every shade of my expression as I blast out of my mind.

I scream louder as he quickens his pace. He drives in harder and delivers a cruel little smashing strike to my ass and thighs each time he fills me with his scorching hot meat.

I cycle higher as he escalates the tension. I can't hold back. He's been bringing me to orgasm since we first walked into this apartment.

I crash into another one and buck up against his thrusts every time he pounds in. He doesn't hold back. He builds to deep, resounding thumps until his body spanks my thighs to full-impact concussions.

I can't look at him anymore. I bury my face in his chest screaming myself hoarse. He husks into my hair and hammers me harder into the couch.

I'm completely losing my mind when he sinks on top of me, stops pounding into me, and starts kissing me for the ages again.

His shaft still rests inside me. He barely moves his hips enough to hold me on tenterhooks, but he doesn't soften. Maybe he never will. Maybe that's his problem—once he starts he can't stop.

I don't know if I can handle a man like this. He turns me on beyond anything I've ever known. He leaves me breathless and he still keeps going.

Each orgasm comes more easily and explodes me farther out of my depths. I need to calm down. Does he understand that? Is that why he slowed down and went back to kissing me again?

He kisses me for what seems like a long time, wraps his arms around me, and holds me and rocks me in a gentle sway. I could easily collapse right now if he wasn't still inside me.

I don't expect him to take this any further. Any second now, he'll pull out, get dressed, and leave. No one has to explain this to me.

So why did he say he doesn't do one-night stands? What is this if it isn't that?

It's still light outside. It isn't even nighttime yet.

He finally breaks off my mouth and shifts over onto the couch next to me. I don't know what he's trying to do until he grabs me behind my knee again, pushes my leg up, and stretches out on the couch behind me.

He keeps me on my back with my leg up while he kisses me and drives into me from behind and below.

The wicked, intoxicating spirals of his hips drive me the rest of the way into space. I whimper in his mouth as crushing orgasms take hold of me. His eyes hover right in front of me, but I can't think. I can't do anything but crumble in his hands.

He flexes his hips in such expert corkscrewing thrusts. He hits every nerve ending up and down my channel.

Every single one of those explosions skyrockets me out of my mind, but I can't scream anymore. This is too intense even for that.

I keep whimpering as the catastrophic waves pummel me into oblivion. His shaft excites me beyond my ability to cope. I don't even know if I can survive this.

The overwhelming power of his presence makes me want to cry. I need so much more of him. How can I ever let him go after this? How can I survive without him giving me this again and again—forever?

He holds my gaze even when I can't focus my vision well enough to match him. He sees me floating into insanity with every powerful thrust.

His breath matches mine rising to tiny hissing gasps. His nostrils flare. Sweat breaks out all over his body, but he only feels more powerful the closer he comes to his own release.

When it happens, he dives in, kisses me once, and then gasps out in broken, tortured breaths right into my mouth. His eyes burst wide open.

He searches me to the depths of my soul for any answers, but I don't even know what the questions are.

I look back into the very bottommost corner of who he is. I want to hear all those questions. I want to know the answers even if we have to search for them together.

His essence floods me. He pumps into me again and again as the last drops of milky goodness eject from him. Then we both collapse on the couch panting, sweating, and totally spent.

Chapter 16: Ethan

I lie on my back in Ivy's bed with my arms around her. She isn't asleep any more than I am.

Her fingers keep occasionally flexing into my sides under my arms where she lies with her arms around me.

I don't have to turn my head to see the illuminated clock on her bedside table. It's four o'clock in the morning and we've been doing it all night—ever since I brought her home from Jake's house.

It was only about three o'clock in the afternoon when I brought her here. We've been locked in this death struggle to consume each other as much as possible before I have to leave.

I don't even know if she has to work today, but I sure as hell do.

I have to make it back to the ranch before the boys come down for breakfast this morning. I can't let them see me doing the walk of shame coming home from Ivy's.

They will never find out what I did with her—not ever. I've never been more certain of anything.

I'm not ashamed of it and I don't regret it. I would do everything the same if I had to do it over again. I might be a little more forceful with her next time—now that I know she wants me as much as I want her.

I just don't want to share this with my brothers. I don't want them to comment on it. I don't want them to say anything about it. I don't want them ever even to know I shared something like this with her.

They all think I'm a monk. They don't know what I've done or who I've gotten involved with or how. I keep that to myself. They don't need to know.

They think I've never had a girlfriend, but the truth is I just never let them find out. Ben, Jack, and Jake can play around all they like. They can joke with the boys about girls they like and what they want to do with them.

My life is my business. It isn't for them to examine under a microscope and decide if it's serious enough for them to treat it with the dignity it deserves.

I could never do that to her. I could never turn her into a joke for the boys to laugh at. She's too beautiful for that.

I don't want to leave, but I have to. I know she'll understand, but it still takes all my effort to roll her onto her back, push myself up on my arms, and glide into her on a river of wetness.

I kiss her once and rear back so I can watch her face spasming with escalating passion.

"I have to go home, baby," I whisper.

"I know!" she gasps.

"You're beautiful," I whisper.

She raises her hand to touch my cheek. "Will I ever see you again—like this, I mean?"

"I don't know, baby. I don't know what's going to happen."

She clamps her eyes shut. "Last night....." She opens them and drowns me in so much emotion I don't know what to do. I can only keep sliding into her, out of her, and into her again. "Thank you," she whispers. "I needed you so much last night."

"Will you be okay—now that Carl is gone? Don't carry this around with you. You did the right thing. You did the world a favor. You have to know that."

She winces again, compresses her lips, and tries to look away, but she only winds up looking up into my eyes again. "You're such a good man. I don't know how you can be so good and still like me."

"Stop," I breathe. "You're perfect. You absolutely did the right thing. You never did anything wrong—with either of them. You can't keep beating yourself up about this. You don't think I should beat myself up for killing those guys in the grocery store...."

"Of course not!"

"There's no difference—except that you never meant to kill either of them—so you're the better person here." I dive in and kiss her.

I don't want to talk anymore, so I pick up my pace. I have to savor this last taste of her body before I leave—maybe forever.

She's impossibly sweet and delicious, but it's her precious heart that makes her so irresistible.

She just wants to do the right thing—for everyone. She wants to do the right thing for me, too.

She kisses me back, and when I break away to watch her again, she doesn't talk.

So much emotion pours out of her eyes when she touches my cheeks. She pets my head and caresses down my neck and chest while I stroke into her.

I see her savoring this last taste of me before I leave, too. She wants me—but she wants more than one night of sex. I understand that now. She wants me—the real me.

I don't want her getting too close. I don't want to shatter the illusion that she thinks I'm a good man.

I wish I could be the man she thinks I am—the man she admires. I wish I could be that so I would be good enough for her, but I'll never be that. She just doesn't know it yet.

She quickens into another whining, gasping orgasm. She doesn't scream the way I made her scream last night.

I can make her scream and thrash and claw at me if I really want to. I can drive her into an animal frenzy where she can't control her own actions.

I don't want to break this moment of contact with her eyes. I don't want her to look away from me even for a second. Driving back to Turning Point is going to be hard enough as it is.

Feeling her saturated, spongy inner tissues clamps around me feels too good. If I don't leave, I'll get stuck here forever.

She drains me to the core again. I can't stand the pressure. I eventually explode into her and collapse into her lips as we both drift in the clouds of Heaven.

I have to go now. Delaying will only make it harder.

I roll off her. She curls onto her side under the covers while I bring my clothes into the bedroom and sit on the bed to get dressed.

She strokes my back and rubs my neck while I put my clothes on, but she doesn't say anything. She already knows.

I kick my feet into my boots and stand up to look down at her while I buckle my belt.

She looks intoxicating lying there with the streetlight streaming across her bed. She's a goddess and she doesn't even know it.

She thinks she's damaged goods because of what she's been through. She doesn't know how perfect she is.

I lean over her and bury my face in her neck before I put my hat on. I inhale a deep lungful of her scent. I have to remember this. I'll dream about this for the rest of my life. I know that now.

I ease off, cup her chin once to kiss her, and walk out before I change my mind.

I fire up my truck and drive off into the darkness. The sun is just coming up when I walk into the ranch house. It's too late for me to take a shower and change my clothes. I don't give a shit anyway.

I go into the kitchen, put on a pot of coffee, and start cooking breakfast. Emma comes down from the bunkhouse first and kisses me on the cheek. "Hey, sweetie," she tells me.

"Hey, baby," I reply. "How's Tati?"

"She isn't any better than she was yesterday morning. I'm going to take her to the Urgent Care Clinic later if she doesn't feel any better."

"I'm sorry to hear that. Is there anything we can do?"

She makes a face. "This has been coming for a long time. The miracle is that she lasted this long considering how she was living before she came to live here."

"Tell Hank to take the day off work if he needs to. He should go with you if you're taking her to the Urgent Care Clinic."

She rolls her eyes to Heaven. "You try to convince him of that. He won't take the day off work. I already tried to convince him, but he won't listen. I even I told him something could happen while we were in town and then he would regret staying behind." She points to the eggs I'm scrambling in the pan. "Do you mind if I take these up to him? I don't want him to leave her until he absolutely has to."

"Go ahead." I dump the eggs onto a plate and add a stack of bacon strips. "I'm making biscuits, but you probably don't want to wait."

She smiles at me. "Maybe later. Thank you, sweetheart." She kisses me again and leaves.

Poor Hank. I might have to say something to Chuck about making Hank stay home from work. He should be with his grandmother.

We've all been counting down the hours before her health started to fail. She's been so sparky and energetic until now.

Everyone loves her. No one wants to see anything happen to her, but she isn't young or healthy anymore. Emma is right. This was inevitable.

I gotta feel for Hank, though. The poor guy must have been dreading this for years.

I get busy replacing the scrambled eggs and frying more bacon. I take the biscuits out of the oven just as Grace comes downstairs with Eli.

She's still wearing her pajamas and bathrobe. She hasn't taken a shower or combed her hair. She looks ten years older.

I frown at her. "You okay, darlin'?"

"This rotten baby is teething again!" she snarls. "He never slept more than a few minutes at a time all night. He's driving me insane!"

I glance behind her. "Where's Wade? He usually stays up with you, doesn't he?"

"He's in the shower on his way down. He did stay up, but I'm on my last nerve." Her features convulse. "I don't know if I can do this anymore, Ethan! I really don't!"

"Here. Give him to me." I take the baby out of her arms and put him against my shoulder. "Go take a shower. Seriously. Get out of here."

She covers her mouth and tears swim in her eyes. She rushes out of the room and leaves me holding Eli.

He doesn't seem too distressed now. He looks around at everything while he gnaws his little fist.

I find myself smirking at him. He's a cherub. Poor Grace. She's been through the mill with a nightmare pregnancy and now taking care of a baby.

I love the little guy, though. He's adorable and he doesn't fuss even once while I cook breakfast with one hand.

My mom and Ava come down next. The boys must all be in the shower, too.

"Hey, baby." My mom frowns at Eli. "Did you just find that on the doorstep or something?"

I try not to smile back at her. "Grace had a bad night. She's taking a break so she can grab a shower. You should help her out today, Mama. She's barely holding on."

"She is?" She glances over her shoulder toward the stairs. "I didn't know that. I would have stuck my nose in earlier if I had known."

"I'm going to have to go to work soon, so maybe you could take him. Try to give her a break today so she can catch up on sleep."

"Okay. I will. Do you want me to take him now?"

I hand off Eli and take my breakfast to the table just as the other boys come downstairs. No one comments on me missing dinner last night.

I was gone way too long just to be dropping off Ivy. I should have at least texted to say I wouldn't be here. Does anyone suspect?

No one treats me like this morning is any different from any other work morning. Everyone is much more concerned about Hank when he finally comes down from the bunkhouse.

He gets tears in his eyes as soon as Wade and Chuck start telling him to take the day off.

"I can't!" he croaks. "I can't stand seeing her like this! I need something to take my mind off it. I'll go crazy if I just have to sit around watching her die!"

"She isn't dying yet, boy." Chuck crushes Hank's shoulder in a death grip. "She's just old—and she loves the crap out of you. If you want to go out with us, you can. I'm sure Emma will call you if anything happens. Then you can leave if you need to."

He nods down at the floor. "Yes, Sir. Thank you."

Everyone tries to play it off like it's no big deal when it is. Everyone tiptoes around Hank on eggshells trying to act normal.

The same enthusiasm doesn't light up the morning the way it usually does. I get lost in the shuffle.

I finish breakfast first since I'm the first one here. I have time to go upstairs, take a quick shower, and change my clothes.

Chapter 17: Ethan

C huck, Hank, Ben, and I drive into Coeur d'Alene to go see the stock sales at the auction yard.

Hank pulls out his phone on the sidewalk and checks it. "Emma is on the way home with Tati. Emma isn't telling me anything serious. I guess it's okay."

"Stop checking your phone," Chuck tells him. "You're supposed to be taking your mind off it. You would have heard if it was anything serious. Now come on. We're going into town. Try to enjoy yourself."

Hank mumbles, "Yes, Sir."

We park down the street and get lost in the crowd at the sale yards. Hank loosens up while we talk about the stock. Chuck is more concerned about bringing in a new bull than replacing the cattle we lost during the recent disease outbreak.

"Why do you even want to bring in a bull of our own?" Ben asks. "Breeding our own cattle will complicate our whole operation. We would have to keep our own cows plus pay for all their veterinary care during gestation—and then we would have a whole bunch of heifer calves that would be useless to us afterward. Why don't we just stick with buying in steer calves and raising them the way we always have?"

Chuck shrugs. "The old man was looking into it when he died. He was doing his research to find out if he could save money doing it the other way. Wade thinks, if the old man considered it, we should be considering it, too. Wade wants to look into it and check the costs. If it's cheaper, it might be worth it. We won't change anything immediately. It would be a slow transition."

"We wouldn't have been able to restock as quickly if we bred our own stock," I point out. "We wouldn't have recovered from the outbreak the way we did. It would have taken ten times longer and cost more—a lot more."

Chuck cocks his head to study me. "You're right. I didn't think of that."

"There are more factors to consider beyond just the operational costs," I tell him. "You might want to mention that to him and take it into consideration."

He looks away. "You're right. I will."

"It isn't like Turning Point hasn't suffered its share of problems these last few years," I go on. "Gestating cows could be a lot more susceptible to freak weather and random disasters—not to mention the stress of wildfires and whatnot. Our herds would be less resilient—more fragile."

He holds up his hand. "You made your point, man. I got it. Now let's pay attention and get the information we came here to get. If you really want to, you can tell Wade all of that yourself."

"He would hear it better from you."

"Don't think I'm going to steal your thunder by making him think they're my ideas. You can tell him yourself. He respects your opinion just as much as mine."

Our conversation dies when the first group of bulls comes out. We don't talk about anything other than the stock after that.

I can't tell if Hank is enjoying himself, but Ben sure does. He makes non-stop comments about all the stock in front of us.

We finally leave and head back to where we parked the trucks. We're just passing the grocery store when Ivy comes out carrying her briefcase and a stack of file folders.

Her eyes dart around the group, lock on me, and then she glances at Ben and the others.

"Look who it is!" he exclaims and bursts into a huge grin. "It's our friendly neighborhood power company rep."

She smiles back at him. "Hi, boys. What brings you to town?"

Ben jerks his thumb over his shoulder. "We were just checking out the slabs of meat over at the sale yards. You should have been there."

She turns bright red and looks away. "I'm sure slabs of meat are your expertise, not mine."

"Did the Police give you any static about the shooting?" Chuck asks. "We didn't hear."

She lowers her eyes. "No, Detective Newcastle was really great about it. I suppose there wasn't a lot to the case once they saw the damage to my car and matching damage on Carl's truck."

"You're damn right there wasn't much to it," he replies. "If they have any issues or give you a hard time, you tell them to talk to us. We'll straight out Rod for you."

She smiles at him, too. "Thank you. I'm beyond grateful to you—all of you—for all your help. I wouldn't be here without you."

"At least you can forget about the deadbeat now, right?" Ben tells her. "You can start living your life, going to all the clubs, and letting your inner wildcat out of its cage."

She blushes at him and tries to look away. "I think you might have me confused with yourself, Ben. I'll see you boys later. Have a good one."

She walks around us and heads off down the street. I don't know what she's driving now—not that it matters.

Ben watches her over his shoulder. Then he faces front, shakes his hand, and whistles. "Damn! She is smoking! Did you see that smile? Dynamite!"

I react without thinking and bump my knuckles against his chest to stop him in his tracks. "What the hell is wrong with you?"

He blinks at me in stunned disbelief. "Uh.....excuse me?"

"You said you weren't interested in her. You said she wasn't your type and you were just being friendly."

"Uh....I was." He glances around at Hank and Chuck.

"Don't you ever flirt with her again. Understand?" I snap. "Treat her like you treat Mama. Be respectful and keep it clean. Understand? I'll be watching."

His jaw drops. I sense Hank and Chuck staring at me, too.

Ben gasps. "What the hell are you talking about?! What difference does it make to you if I flirt with her or not—or if I'm interested in her?"

"Just don't do it," I snap. "You've already made an ass of yourself enough where she's concerned. Quit while you're ahead and conduct yourself like a grown man instead of a prepubescent toddler. Don't let me catch you stepping out of line with her again or you'll deal with me. Do you got that?"

He shuts his mouth with difficulty. "Uh.....yes, Sir. I got it."

"Good," I snap. "Now let's go."

I turn my back on them. I don't want to see Hank and Chuck looking at me like that.

I could stand Ben looking at me like that, but not Chuck. He knows me too well. He sees all and knows all.

I probably shouldn't have said that. Now all three of them will start to suspect there's something going on between me and Ivy.

There is nothing going on between me and Ivy. I don't know why I warned Ben away from her. I've never warned him away from any other woman.

I stay ahead of them all the way back to the trucks. I don't talk to any of them before I get in and drive back to the ranch.

We meet up at the house. Hank goes straight to the bunkhouse without talking to anyone. Chuck heads for the old man's office to tell Wade what we found out at the sale yards.

That leaves me alone with Ben. He keeps giving me side looks, but he doesn't broach the subject of Ivy, thank the stars.

I keep myself busy with ranch business until dinner rolls around. I don't go anywhere I might have to deal with him.

I'm more furious at him than I am at myself for snapping at him. He better not start disrespecting Ivy.

I don't care what's going on between us or even if anything is going on between us. I don't care if she's nothing but our power company rep.

He owes her respect even if she's only that. He's acting like a child the way he flirts with her all the time.

He acts like it's open season on her because she's one of the very few single youngish black women in the area.

That doesn't make her bait for guys like him. This has nothing to do with whether there's anything going on between me and her. I won't stand by and let him treat her like that.

I have to deal with him at dinnertime. At least I don't have to sit near him.

The family spends almost the entire meal talking about Hank's Tati and what might be wrong with her.

"The doctors say it's just a seasonal cold-like virus and we just have to ride it out," Emma tells us. "It isn't critical yet, so we just have to wait and see if it gets any worse before they can do anything about it."

I glance over at Hank. He pushes the food around on his plate and doesn't look at or talk to anyone. Jesus, he looks so sad!

"Everything will work out, Hank," Liza tells him. "She'll recover from this."

He doesn't respond. He shows no sign that he even hears her.

It doesn't matter if Mrs. Pendergrass recovers from this. If this doesn't kill her, something else will. She's too old and not in the greatest shape.

This is the beginning of the end. Hank must be realizing that now. He really does have to stand by and watch his grandmother die. All the doctors in the world can't stop it.

Chuck and Wade change the subject by talking about the sales and the livestock at the yards. They're in the middle of their conversation when Hank puts his fork down too hard.

He barely chokes out, "May I please be excused, Ma'am?"

My mom says, "Of course, baby. Try to get some sleep tonight, okay?"

He kicks back his chair too fast and blunders out of the house. A hush falls over the room until the door slams shut.

"Do you want to go, too, sweetheart?" my mom asks Emma.

"I don't think it will make any difference. He might just want to be alone for a while. I think I better stay here."

"Whatever works for you." My mom goes back to eating.

Ben must be smarting from my comments because he takes that opportunity to double down in front of everyone.

"Ethan got his first girlfriend," he announces.

Gasps and exclamations race around the table. "He did not!" Jack counters.

"Who is it?" Ava shuts her eyes and holds up her hand. "Let me rephrase that. Who do you say it is, Ben?"

"Ivy Harper, the power company rep," Ben replies and shoots me a snarky grin down the table. "He's sweet on her."

My mom squeezes my arm. "This is wonderful! She's such a nice girl. You should invite her over for dinner again. I like her."

"Is that true, Ethan?" Wade asks. "Why didn't you tell us what was going on?"

"He didn't tell us because there is nothing going on," Chuck interrupts. "Ben has been huffing the diesel fumes again."

Laughter breaks out around the table. Nathan elbows Ben extra hard and makes him laugh.

My mom turns to me. "Go on. Tell us. When did this happen?"

"Nothing happened and there's nothing going on," I tell her. "I drove her home after the shooting yesterday. That's all."

Her face falls. "Oh. Are you saying Ben made it all up?"

"I didn't make it all up, did I?" Ben counters. "He warned me to stay away from her and never flirt with her again. That should tell you all you need to know."

His tone snaps my temper, but this time, I manage to keep myself under a tight rein. "Isn't it enough that she's been on the run from a dangerous stalker and just shot the guy when he was trying to kill her? Do you really have to make her life more difficult than it already is so you can toy with her for your own entertainment? Is that really the person the old man raised you to be? Don't you have any respect at all for what she's going through? If you were there yesterday and saw how upset she was about getting her damn car run into a ravine with her inside it and then some armed madman coming after her and trying to shoot her in the head, maybe you would have a little more respect and stop treating her like a piece of ass standing on the street corner."

Dead silence falls over the dinner table. The old man never would have tolerated any of his children using profanity at the dinner table, but Ben's attitude is more than I can stand.

He has always been the other half of me. I never let anything come between us, but I can't let him talk about her like that—or treat her like that.

Wade doesn't tell me to clean up my language. It would be his place as head of the family to pull me into line if I stepped out of it.

He doesn't say anything and neither does my mom. No one says a word. Ben looks away first and stares down into his plate. Good. He better think twice if he wants to talk shit about Ivy.

Chapter 18: Ivy

I look up from my desk and freeze when I see Wade, Jake, and Gabe Crenshaw and Nolan Dewey walking into the power company's main headquarters office.

"Hello!" I exclaim. "What brings you here?"

"We got called in for a meeting about the upgrades," Wade replies. "Do you mean you don't know about it?"

"I never heard anything about it after we talked and you signed off on it." I frown at him. "What is this about?"

"We were hoping you could tell us," Jake replies. "The person who called said the planned upgrades aren't sufficient for our power needs and the company needs to reevaluate the whole project."

"They're slapping us with another twenty-thousand-dollar tab for the new improvements," Wade adds. "Could you look into it before the meeting? Just give us a clue what we're dealing with here."

"Sure." I wave behind me. "Come into my office."

I lead them inside. Wade and Jake sit in the chairs in front of my desk. Gabe sits in a different chair off to one side.

Nolan stands by the door and leans his shoulder against the door frame. He doesn't join in the conversation.

I look up the Turning Point Ranch Trust electricity account on my computer and scroll through the documentation. It takes me way too long to find what I'm looking for.

When I do, I frown at the documents trying to understand what I'm seeing.

"What's wrong?" Wade asks. "Now I'm worried."

I shake my head trying to clear my thoughts. "This is really weird. The company has already slated you for the second tier of upgrades."

"What does that mean?" Gabe asks.

"It means someone is trying to pull a fast one on you. These upgrades aren't usually covered by insurance policies. This meeting you're about to have—someone is going to try to strong-arm you into agreeing to the second tier of upgrades—but you have no reason to accept them. They're completely voluntary—and I would say unnecessary based on your power consumption needs. The first tier of upgrades—the ones I already discussed with you—they should be more than adequate."

"So what should we do in this meeting?" Jake asks.

"Just put your foot down and flatly refuse to accept the upgrades—and don't sign anything, not even a waiver of liability. That's an old trick. Just tell whoever is negotiating with you that you only signed off on the first tier. Tell them that, if they install the second tier and try to charge you later, you'll take them to court. Tell them in no uncertain terms that you absolutely refuse the second tier of upgrades. Tell that that you'll be checking with the repair crew when they come out to your property. If the repair crew plans to install the second tier of upgrades anyway, you'll take the company to court for that, too."

Wade frowns. "Will that work?"

"The company can't legally install the second tier of upgrades without your signature on a piece of paper. Just flatly refuse to give your permission to anything other than what you've already signed off on. If the repair crew comes out to the ranch saying they're ready to install the second tier, then you should deny them access and threaten to have them arrested for criminal trespass if they don't leave immediately."

The three brothers exchange glances. "Wow," Wade murmurs. "This is serious."

"Not really. Just stand your ground and assert your legal rights." I glance at the computer and shake my head again. "I can't believe they're actually trying to pull this crap."

"Why are they doing it?" Gabe asks. "They can't be doing it for the money."

I make a face. "I don't know why they're doing it, but as soon as you leave my office, I'm going to go through the whole database and contact everyone else who has this on their account. This is criminal. If we don't stop it, the whole company could be in hot water."

"Thank you, Ivy," Wade exclaims. "We owe you big time for this."

I grin at him. "Let's call it even after everything your family has done for me." I stand up. "We better get going. Your meeting is about to start."

I accompany the four men down the hall toward the conference room where the company reps always hold meetings with customers.

I'm just about to turn to Wade and the others and wish them good luck. I freeze when I see Ethan through the building's front windows.

He stands on the sidewalk in front of the building, leans his shoulder against a lamppost, and faces out into the street with his back to the building entrance. He doesn't turn around.

He couldn't make it more obvious why he's here and why he's standing in that position. He doesn't want to see me. He doesn't even want to take the chance that he might see me.

A million thoughts and ideas tumble through my head. Why did he spend the night with me at all if he just plans to avoid me?

He said he doesn't do one-night stands, but that's exactly what he's turning this into. Does he ever plan to look at me or talk to me ever again?

Why did he act so kind and loving then and now he won't even risk seeing me from a distance?

"What did you do to him?" Jake asks.

I snap out of my trance and spin around. "Huh? I didn't do anything to him."

"Something is under his skin," Wade remarks. "I don't know what it is if it isn't you. He warned Ben to stay away from you, so something is going on with him. He's never acted this way about any woman before—not that any of us can remember."

I don't know what to say, but right then, the company reps come out of the conference room.

"Mr. Crenshaw?" one of them asks.

Wade, Jake, and Gabe all turn around to deal with the guy. Then they all go into the conference room and leave me standing there.

Ethan doesn't turn around once. He doesn't even know I'm here.

I walk back to my office seething in confusion and turmoil. I don't know what he meant to do that night or why he did it, but it must not have meant as much to him as it did to me.

Someone that closed off can't be good for me. He must have been telling the truth when he said it wasn't a good idea for us to get involved.

I'll just have to take him at his word and put it behind me. He gave me one of the greatest nights of my life, but now it's over. Whatever we shared that night won't come back and neither will he.

I concentrate on work and I don't see any of the Crenshaws after their meeting. I have enough to worry about contacting everyone with the second tier of upgrades listed on their accounts.

I lodge a formal complaint with the company corporate team. They might be the ones behind this—or some lower-level manager or executive might have implemented this strategy on their own.

I'm covering my bases one way or the other. I can't let the company screw over good people like this—and for what? For a fistful of dollars? It makes no sense at all.

I barely get through the database by the end of the day—like I have nothing more important to deal with.

I gather up a bunch of my case files to work on at home. Now I'm behind on my regular work schedule.

I head out to my car, stop by the grocery store, and then go to the hardware store. I have to fix the doorjamb of my duplex. Carl damaged it when he kicked in the door.

I'm just coming out of the hardware store and sticking my key into the driver's door to unlock my car when I spot Ethan across the street.

He stands alone in the cemetery. His truck sits parked at the curb. None of the other Crenshaws are anywhere nearby. He's completely alone.

I can't see from here which grave he's standing at—like it's any of my business.

I start to look down at my key again. He obviously wants to be alone—and he obviously doesn't want to see me.

I'm a split second away from taking my eyes off him when he looks up and sees me. I immediately look away, but it's too late.

At least he can see me parked in the hardware store parking lot with my purchases in my hand. He can see I wasn't following him. I just happened to randomly spot him from a distance.

I get busy unlocking my door to get into the driver's seat. The sooner I leave, the better.

I start to open the door—and my heart stops when I see him coming toward me. Now what is he going to do?

He would never put me in danger. I know that even if I don't know anything else about him.

I'm more concerned about making him uncomfortable, but he doesn't seem to have that problem right now. He walks right up to me—on this side of the car.

"Hey," he mumbles under his breath.

"Hey. What's up? Are you okay?"

He waves behind him. He won't look me in the eye. "Yeah...I was just...you know....visiting my old man."

I study him a little closer. Of course it would be that. "I mean it. Are you okay?"

He squints across the street in the other direction. "I'm really sorry.....that I've been so distant.... "

"Don't worry about it," I tell him. "You told me it wasn't a good idea for us to get involved and you were right. You obviously have your own stuff to deal with. Let's just forget the whole thing ever happened. I'm really grateful for all your help, but we don't have to take it any further."

"It isn't that," he murmurs down at the ground. "All my life....I made it my business to take care of Ben. I never let myself have a life of my own. I don't really know how to."

"Don't you think it's time you changed that? Ben is a grown man. He can take care of himself."

"I know. I just...I don't know if I *can* change it. I don't know how to do that, either." Is he gulping? "I'm not who you think I am."

I raise my hand. "Listen. This whole thing....it's a really bad idea. You obviously aren't ready for something like this and I'm not exactly relationship material, either. You know the worst thing about me. I don't blame you for not wanting to get involved with that."

"It isn't that," he counters a little more forcefully.

"Then what is it? Just tell me the truth."

He looks away and opens his mouth, but no sound comes out.

I turn back to my car. "I better go. You're too closed off from me. I can't keep fighting you to get you to open up. If you don't want to tell me, you'll just have to keep carrying it alone. Have a good one, Ethan."

He steps forward too fast and snaps, "Stop!"

He sticks his arm between me and the car, but he doesn't go as far as actually restraining me.

He backs off immediately and raises both hands as if to show me that he's harmless. "Don't leave, Ivy. Please. Don't leave."

"Give me one reason why I shouldn't. You're the one who has been holding me at a distance. If you don't want to do this—if you won't even look at me—I'm not going to make you do it. Just go your own way and leave me alone."

He backs off again and waves behind him. "Please....just come with me.....just for a few minutes. If you still want to leave, I won't ever talk to you again. I swear it. Just a few minutes. That's all I'm asking."

I study him. Is he finally ready to open himself up to me? Don't I owe him at least that much consideration?

I put my hardware purchases in the car and shut the door. "All right," I tell him. "Where do you want me to go?"

Chapter 19: Ivy

Ethan doesn't speak on our way back across the street. He won't even look at me when we reenter the cemetery.

He passes Tom Crenshaw's grave like it isn't even there. Ethan keeps going between the rows to the very back of the cemetery.

He stops in front of two simple, plain, ordinary gravestones with no decoration and no flowers on them.

The names on the stones are, *Jax Ingram*, and *Trisha Ingram*. They both have the same death date.

My blood runs cold when I realize. These are the graves of Ben's and Ethan's parents.

He bows his head and looks down at his hands. He keeps kneading his thumbs into his palms in nervous agitation. He hides his eyes under his hat so he won't see me or anything else.

"They didn't get killed by thieves," he husks. "I was four years old and I remember everything that happened that night. Ben was one. He was lying on his back in his crib and I was standing across the room by the door when it happened. Ben was crying. I remember he cried a lot. He was always crying. My mother went over to his crib. She stood over him and raised a knife. She was about to stab Ben. My father always kept a loaded gun in the drawer of the table by the couch. I used to watch him clean it, load it, and put it back in the drawer. He always told me, 'If any bad guys ever come into the house, you take that gun and shoot them. Understand?' My mother was always sweet and loving toward me. She adored my father—and then she had Ben. She went out of her mind. She used to go into these rages and she never showered or brushed her hair. I remember thinking she turned into a monster—and she was about to kill Ben. I didn't even recognize my own mother. I thought she was one of the bad guys—so I pulled out the gun and shot her with it."

I can't move. I can't even breathe. A four-year-old boy.....went through that nightmare

"The shot hit her in the chest. She fell over and the knife fell out of her hand. I couldn't think of anything except that Ben wasn't in danger anymore. My father was in the other room. He came in, saw my mother, and came at me. His face twisted up and he looked like a monster, too. I thought he must be one of the bad guys about to grab me. I fired again and the shot hit him in the head. He fell over and landed on the floor next to my mother."

I gasp out, "Jesus, Ethan!"

"I didn't know what to do. My father always liked to watch crime shows on TV, so I knew what fingerprints were. I rubbed the gun down, put it back in the drawer, and went back to bed. I pretended to be asleep until the Police woke me up."

I don't know what to say. Looking at Ethan hurts—but not as much as he must have been hurting carrying this around all these years.

No wonder he's so distant and serious.

"No one knows," he croaks. "Ben doesn't know. I never told anyone. Everyone thinks intruders broke into the house and killed my parents. The Crenshaws never questioned it. I let everyone believe I didn't remember anything from that night."

I take a few steps closer to him. No wonder it took so much for him to tell me. Of course he pushed me away.

Before I can get near him, his head shoots up and he locks his eyes on me. They don't look ferocious or flinty or even determined anymore. He just looks haunted and deeply anguished over this burden he's been carrying all these years.

"You can't tell anyone," he rasps. "You can never tell anyone, especially not Ben."

"I won't tell anyone. I'm honored that you confided in me."

He lowers his hat brim in front of his eyes again. "I'm just....poisoned....by everything. I don't know how anyone can ever love me. The only people who love me don't know the truth. They wouldn't have anything to do with me if they knew. I can't even accept the love of my own family because they don't know. None of them know who I really am."

I can't listen to this. I cross the grass and slip my hand into his. "I know who you really are....and I still want you. I feel poisoned, too. I feel like no one would ever really want me if they knew about me." I find myself looking away to hide a sudden pang of anguish. "I don't blame you for keeping away from me. I'm bad news."

"No, you aren't!" His head shoots up. "You killed those men to protect yourself! You aren't poisoned—not at all. If anything, shooting them makes you more pure."

"You killed your parents to protect yourself, too. Don't you see? You did it to protect Ben and yourself. This is no different from shooting those men in the grocery store. That's what you've been telling me all this time."

He winces and looks away, but he doesn't take his hand out of mine. "I don't know if I can accept that."

"You're thinking about this as a four-year-old boy. You're see this from the point of view of when you made the decision to wipe those prints and hide the truth from the Police. Imagine if this happened to some other child—someone you don't know. Who you are as an adult would tell that child that they did the right thing—the same way you've been telling me that I did the right thing. I don't see any difference."

He shakes his head. "I know you're right, but I just can't get it out of my head. I've been living with this for too long."

I take my hand out of his, close his cheeks in both my palms around both his cheeks, and turn him toward me so I can kiss him.

"If you're poison, then so am I," I tell him. "You don't have to worry about poisoning me because I'm already poisoned by my own nightmares. If you say I'm not, then you aren't, either. You don't have to protect Ben anymore. You deserve a life of your own where you can be happy without carrying this around. I know who you are and I still want you. You can come with me right now or you can walk away. I'll accept your decision, but I won't wait around for you to decide."

He really does swallow then. "Are you sure about this?"

"Of course I'm sure. You're the best man I've ever known, but if you don't want me...."

"I do want you," he blurts out. "Don't you know that by now?"

I shrug. "You apparently don't want me enough to take me—and that's okay. It's the same thing in the end. Did you really think I would turn away from you because of this? You do what you want. I don't need to wait around for a man who won't come to me when he knows it's right."

I turn away to leave. I might be being heartless toward him when he just bared his soul and told me his worst secret, but I have to take care of myself.

He isn't the man I think he is if he isn't man enough to take the woman he wants when she's standing right in front of him.

He grabs my arm hard to spin me back around—and the next thing I know, we're kissing as never before. His arms lock around me and his mouth devours my lips in torrential madness.

He's never kissed me like this before. No one ever has.

He inhales me and clenches his fist in my clothes—in my jacket behind my back, on my hip, behind my neck, and then he grabs my ass.

He attacks me harder, faster, and more ravenously than ever. He never let his desire show this much before. He never let it show at all.

His hands and mouth communicate so much buried need—so much volcanic hunger for something he never lets himself have.

He kisses me much longer and much harder than I would have kissed him. He keeps going long after I would have broken away.

He doesn't let go of me even when he does ease off. He stays right in close to my face stroking my cheeks and stealing little pecks on my lips while he stares deep into my eyes.

I don't know what he's thinking or what will happen next. I only know the barrier is down now. Whatever wall separated us before no longer exists.

He finally relaxes his grip on me and pulls my clothes straight. He looks down at my body while he does it—like he's responsible for making sure I look right.

"I'll see you back at your place," he murmurs. "Okay?"

I nod in breathless amazement. I can't even smile—not when he looks at me like that. I can only whisper, "Okay."

Chapter 20: Ethan

I tremble when I reenter Ivy's apartment. I told myself I would never come back here.

Now she knows about me and she still wants me. I don't know what will happen between us, but I can't let her slip through my fingers.

I don't regret telling her. I just don't know who I am or what my life is—now that someone in the world knows the truth.

I've been living with this alone for so long. I'm not alone anymore and it scares the shit out of me.

I hold it together until she shuts the door behind her. It's barely evening. I should ask her out to dinner or something.

She waves toward the couch. "Sit down," she tells me.

I sit down and she sits next to me. I don't know what to do next. I'm no good at stuff like this.

I never let myself get close to any girl before. I never let myself get serious about anyone.

Part of me always knew that getting serious meant telling the truth. I couldn't get involved with someone without them knowing who and what I really am.

She slips her hand into mine and squeezes. She smiles at me when I look up. "Do you want something to drink?" she asks.

I want something to drink, but it isn't anything she can get me from the kitchen.

I lean across the couch and kiss her again. I never want to stop—not ever.

I want to keep feeling her lips soften....and her tongue slithering around mine.....

I want to feel her body easing toward me....and her round, voluptuous breasts falling into my hands.....and her ass arching when I squeeze up her thighs......

She moans into my mouth when I massage her breasts through her blouse. Her legs spread when I grip her knees and pull her thighs apart.

That's where I belong—deep in her darkest recesses. I can hide in there and find some blessed relief from being on the outside all this time.

She collapses into my arms. I pick her up and sit her sideways on my lap the way I did before. She rocks in my embrace. Her head falls onto my shoulder while we kiss.

She rotates her choice round ass into my package and drives me wild. I'm going to take her tonight—and I won't hold back this time.

I squeeze up between her thighs and duck my hand under her skirt. She mews into my mouth when I rub her through her wet panties.

She rides her hips against my hand until I slip my fingers inside her. She undulates in a seductive rhythm taking my hand all the way in. Oh yeah.

She makes me so damn hard it hurts, but I want that. I want to break her in half and feel her cave underneath me.

Her delicious scent blasts my mind apart when she bucks and screams in excruciating orgasm. Her body heaves against my hand and her succulent juices gush down my fingers. I have to taste that. I have to experience that.

I sit her up planning to lie her down and eat her to kingdom come. As soon as she sits up, though, something changes.

I turn her away from me and pull up her skirt. She arches back against my package in such a suggestive riding movement that I can't resist.

I pull her skirt the rest of the way up and pull her panties aside. Her ass swells in front of me when she rides back and then contracts when she drills down hard on my prick.

I groan at the intensity of that sensation. I need to get inside her.

She doesn't try to turn around. She plants her hands on my knees, leans forward, and turns her head slightly to show me her back rocking on top of me.

I grab my belt and rip open my fly. She doesn't stop me from rubbing my stiff meat against her dripping slit.

She squeals when I press it in on her next back stroke. She takes it and then backs all the way up to ride me full force.

All the raving madness of that first night comes back with a vengeance. I need her like this. I need to see her sighing and moaning in rapture while she grinds her sweet box all the way on top of me.

My hands find her hips. She matches my movements perfectly and complies when I pull her back into my rhythm.

I love the feel of my hand sliding up her spine and bending her farther forward. She leans over my knees. Her breasts bulge between her arms.

I want to see her exposed and raw before me. I grab her jacket and blouse, ripe them back off her shoulders, and her breasts fall out in front of her.

I pinch her nipples and make her moan when she sinks back down on top of me. Her body possesses so many delights for me to discover—but she's right here in my hands. I don't have to go looking for her anymore.

Even hours later when we lie exhausted and satisfied in each other's arms, I still see her like that. I see her uncovering all her hidden mysteries for me.

I'm the only man who has ever seen her like that. She doesn't have to tell me. She never shared this with her late husband.

He didn't know her well enough to unlock this part of her. He couldn't have if he would actually raise a weapon to threaten her.

He couldn't possibly have known what a prize she is—and now she's mine.

I slip out of the apartment while she sleeps and drive back to Turning Point. I get there just as the boys are coming downstairs for breakfast.

"Where the hell have you been?" Wade demands. "You can't just keep disappearing off the face of the Earth and not tell us where you are and when you're coming back!"

"I'm back now." I look around. "What are we doing today?"

He glares at me. "Where were you?"

"None of your business. Do you mind? I'm hungry."

I sidestep him and head for the kitchen. The rest of the family stands around watching me and waiting to hear me explain myself.

I don't. I never have to explain myself ever again to anyone.

Chuck doesn't get involved in questioning me. His eyes go hard watching me evade Wade's questions.

Chuck knows too much to ask the same questions again. If I didn't answer Wade, I won't answer Chuck or anyone else.

We go out to work, but I leave early without telling anyone where I'm going.

I drive back to Ivy's apartment and find her sitting on the couch in a casual skirt, button-up blouse, and a short, casual black denim jacket with the sleeves half rolled up.

She shoots to her feet as soon as I walk in the door. "Are you sure you want to do this?" she asks.

"Of course. It will be fine. Come on. You have nothing to worry about."

I put her in my truck and hold hands with her while I drive her back to Turning Point. Wade gives me a dirty look in the driveway and then everyone stops what they're doing when they see me open the passenger door to let Ivy out.

I don't pay any attention to any of them. I lead Ivy into the house and let my mom and the girls take over.

My mom welcomes Ivy with all the warmth and enthusiasm I expect. The girls are all thrilled to see Ivy again. Even Mrs. Pendergrass is feeling good enough to come down to the ranch house for dinner.

None of my brothers asks me anymore what's going on or where I've been disappearing to. Everybody knows now.

Ben hangs back and barely says a word to me or Ivy. He conducts himself perfectly all evening. No one would ever guess he ever flirted with her or expressed any interest in her.

My mom sits Ivy next to me at the end of the table. I always sit next to my mom. Now Ivy takes that place and sits between us.

Even that seems so fitting. I love my mom, but someone else was always bound to take her place.

The same flow of conversation sweeps up and down the table. Ivy gets pulled into conversation about the damage from the electrical storms and all the upgrades and repairs going on all over the area.

The others talk as much about ranch business. No one acts like Ivy's presence changes anything—because it doesn't.

Ben, Jack, and Chuck are the only men here who aren't paired off with someone. Why should I be any different?

Ivy and my mom talk about Ivy's family back in North Carolina.

"My sister and her husband moved to France three years ago," Ivy replies. "I barely ever hear from them. I think my sister went native. I don't think her children even speak English."

"Are your parents still back in North Carolina?" my mom asks.

"My father is in a nursing home with dementia. He doesn't recognize me anymore. I went to visit him the last time about two years ago and we said our goodbyes—or I did. He never even found out that I married Carl. My mom has been gone for more than ten years. My dad and my sister are my only family, so I don't really have any reason to go back. I really don't want to see my dad again. The man I loved is already gone. Seeing a dead body sitting up in a chair only makes me m ad."

My mom squeezes her arm. "I understand. No one should have to go through that."

I'm just deciding if I should change the subject when we hear a car drive up in the driveway. Chuck cocks his ear to listen. Then he stands up to go see who it is.

Someone climbs up to the porch and knocks on the front door before he gets there. He opens it and finds two men standing outside.

One is an old man with frizzy white hair and thick glasses. He squints through them to examine Chuck, but I don't think the old man even realizes the person who is standing in front of him.

The second man is much younger. He can't be out of his twenties and he's much taller than the old man. The young guy wears his brown hair cut short and hangs back to let the old man do all the talking.

"Good evening, young man," the old man croaks. "Would you be either Ben or Ethan Ingram?"

"No, I wouldn't be," Chuck returns in his fiercest growl. "Can I help you? This is private property. What are you doing here?"

"Well...." The old man rummages in a leather business satchel next to him, gets confused, and turns to the younger man.

The younger man hands his older companion a file folder. The old man gets confused trying to open it, read it, and address Chuck at the same time.

"I'm trying to find Ben and Ethan Ingram, you see," the old man quavers. "I thought this was their address, but I may have gotten it wrong. Would you happen to know where I can find them?"

"They do live here," Chuck returns in his usual cutting tone. " But I'm not letting you see them until you tell me why you're here. State your business or be on your way."

"Just let them in," Wade yells over. "They don't look dangerous."

Chuck glares at the old man, but the old guy can't see well enough to understand that facial expression.

Chuck stands aside and I get to my feet to face the two men as they walk into the house.

"I'm Ethan Ingram," I tell the old man. "Can I help you with something?"

He bursts into a huge grin. "Ah, yes! Of course. You're so much bigger than I expected."

"You aren't," I tell him.

He bursts into musical laughter and goes through another bout of confusion trying to put his satchel down and open the file folder at the same time.

"I'm Bernard Kershaw." The old man waves to the young man next to him. "This my grandson, Patrick Kershaw. We're attorneys at law representing your grandparents' estate, you see. Your grandfather died five years ago. He was the last surviving relative of the....."

He struggles through another flurry of useless movements.

I glance at my mom. "Which grandfather are you talking about? My grandfather has been dead for more than thirty years."

He laughs again like I just made the biggest joke in history. "Not that grandfather! I'm talking about your maternal grandfather—your other maternal grandfather—Josiah Montague—your mother's father—your biological mother."

I glance at my mom again. Everyone else at the table is already on their feet and gathering around to listen.

"What about him?" I ask. "I never knew him."

"No, of course not! I understand the whole story, you see. Of course we all know about the tragedy with your parents and all. Such a terrible state of affairs...."

"Could you just tell us what this is about?" Ben interrupts. "What does this have to do with our biological parents?"

"You see....your grandparents—your maternal grandparents—your biological maternal grandparents, I mean—they were actually quite wealthy. They owned considerable property in the area....including Hollow River Hill Ranch...I believe it's just down the road from here."

The rest of us exchange glances. Hollow River Hill is between Eastwood and Iron Mountain.

Eastwood and Iron Mountain adjoin along one boundary line. The other adjoining ranch is Hollow River Hill.

"You see....your grandparents owned the ranch....but of course your biological parents didn't ranch. They rented an apartment in Coeur d'Alene—which is where you and your brother were born. Your grandparents leased the ranch to other parties over the years—and then your grandparents died. Your grandfather's will leaves his estate to any of his surviving blood descendants—but you and your brother are the only surviving blood descendants. It's taken us this long just to find you." He bursts out laughing again. "We would have come sooner if we knew where you were."

I blink at him in stunned shock. Hollow River Hill Ranch.....is ours.....mine and Ben's?

My mom steps forward. "Are you sure there isn't some mistake about this? The social service did extensive research to try to find any of Ben's and Ethan's blood relatives when their parents first died. The social workers only placed the boys with us temporarily in case some relatives came forward who wanted to take the boys instead. They only stayed with us because there was no one else."

Bernard laughs again. "Yes, I know all about it! You see, Mr. Montague Senior didn't even know his daughter had any children. They had a terrible falling out before she met and married Jax Ingram. She didn't speak to her father again in this life, so he didn't know he had any grandsons." He turns to me. "I'm certain he would have raised you as his own if he knew."

I can't listen to this. I turn away and walk out of the house. I need to get as far away from this information as possible.

Chapter 21: Ivy

The door slams extra loudly when Ethan walks out of the Turning Point Ranch house without a word of explanation to anyone.

A hush falls over the room—and then I glance over at Ben. He stares at Bernard Kershaw in a trance. Ben barely even sees the guy.

Wade saves the situation by stepping forward. "What do Ben and Ethan need to do to accept their inheritance? Is that why you're here—to get them to sign something?"

"No, no!" Bernard laughs again. "We don't have the authority to do that. We need to meet with both brothers at the courthouse in town. We'll sign the title transfers there and also transfer control of Mr. Montague's bank accounts....."

Ben stumbles away from the table and collapses on the couch with his back to the room.

Wade takes over. "When should they meet you? Do they need to set a time and day?"

"That would be wonderful." Bernard takes a business card out of his pocket. "Call that number there and my receptionist will arrange a time convenient for everyone."

He glances around the room and the cheery smile drains off his face. Neither of the men he came to see are here anymore. Ben doesn't turn around and Ethan isn't here at all.

Wade distracts Bernard by sticking out his hand. "Thank you for coming out to see us, Sir. We'll call you in the next day or two and arrange all of this. Thank you again. We really appreciate your diligence in this matter."

His presence brings Bernard back to his senses. Bernard smiles again, shakes hands, and he and Patrick leave.

Camille glances across the room at Ben. "I don't know about this...."

"I better go see if I can find Ethan." I turn away. "I'll come back and touch base with you before I go home."

I race out of the house. I don't know where Ethan is. He could have disappeared onto the ranch where I'll never find him.

I walk out of the house and spot him hiking up a high hill behind the house. He's already a long way off.

I have to run my hardest to catch up with him. Even then, he outpaces me. My legs and chest hurt by the time I get near him.

I only catch up with him at all because he stops on another hilltop out of sight from the ranch house. He stops there and squats down in the long grass to gaze down the hill to the landscape on the other side.

I flop down in the grass next to him. "He's gone," I pant. "Bernard is gone."

He doesn't turn around to look at me. "I don't want it. Ben can have it."

"That's okay. You don't have to accept it."

He turns his head farther away. "My grandfather wouldn't have taken us if he knew the truth. None of them would have. Mama and the old man wouldn't have taken us if they knew about me, either. They think I'm the victim in all of this."

I squeeze his arm right above the wrist. "Ben is alive now because of you. You said you dedicated your whole life to taking care of him and protecting him. You killed those guys in the grocery store because they threatened him. Don't you see? You did protect him. You can't tell me that was a mistake. Don't tell me you would trade your brother's life for some lunatic who tried to kill him."

He doesn't answer.

"You were right, Ethan," I tell him. "Your mother was one of the bad guys. She was one of the bad guys in that moment. She might have been out of her mind, but she was dangerous to Ben and to you. She was a monster and she went out of her mind. So was your father. You took care of yourself and Ben."

"I still don't want this. I won't take it."

I take a minute to think about that. I don't want to contradict him. He doesn't have to accept his inheritance if he really doesn't want it.

I can understand why inheriting his own ranch might just be rubbing salt into the wound. He already feels bad enough about killing his parents.

He's only inheriting this property because they aren't around to inherit it in his place. That probably makes him feel even guiltier.

"You don't have to take the ranch," I tell him. "Why don't you put it into the family trust? One of your brothers could work the land and live in the ranch house. It doesn't have to be you or Ben, but the property can still benefit the Crenshaws. Isn't that what you want? Wouldn't you want this inheritance to help out the Crenshaws after they gave you this life?"

"Of course," he murmurs.

I put my arm around his shoulders and rest my head against him. He's as big and solid as ever—and now I know he's serious about me.

He brought me home to have dinner with his family. I've been here before, but this is different. He really must be serious if he did this.

He turns his head, kisses the top of my hair, and nuzzles his cheek into my scalp.

"I don't know how to do this," he chokes. "I never let myself do relationships because.....I didn't want it to turn into my parents."

"We'll work it out," I tell him. "It won't turn into that because you won't let it—and I won't let it."

I look up at him, but he won't look at me.

"Would you ever do to me what Trey did?" I ask.

"Of course not," he murmurs. "Never."

"And I would never do what your mother did. We're both on watch for that now. I wouldn't get together with you if you were like Trey and you wouldn't get together with me if I was like your mother." I lean and kiss him on the neck. "She wasn't your mother and he wasn't your father. Your parents are Tom and Camille Crenshaw. Our relationship will be like theirs. That's all you need to know."

His face spasms once. He barely makes a sound when he croaks, "Thank you—for all of this."

"You're the one who gave me this. You're the one who did all of this by being such a good man. You're a good man because you learned from the best. You said so yourself. Everybody says so. You won't be like your parents. You'll be Tom."

I wait a long time, but he doesn't speak again. We sit next to each other just staring out at the view. It's starting to get dark and the wind gets cold.

I take his hand. "Let's go back to the house. You don't have to rush into any decisions about what to do with the ranch. You should probably talk to Ben about it—and your brothers. This affects everyone, so Wade and Chuck will probably have something to say about it, too."

He nods and doesn't fight it when I pull him to his feet. We walk back to the ranch house much more calmly.

He splits away as soon as we walk in the door. He heads upstairs to his room, but not before he tells me he'll be right back to drive me home. The others are all cleaning up the dinner table. I try to help out, but they won't let me.

I head out to the living room to say my goodbyes to Camille and the others. I'm just hugging Liza and Ava when Ben comes over to me.

I realize in that moment that no one else is around. All the other conversations take place in different parts of the living room. Ben and I are alone.

He doesn't laugh or joke around or even smile at me. He actually looks upset. "I hope you don't mind, Ivy," he blurts out. "I need to talk to you about Ethan."

"Uh...okay. What would you like to talk about?"

"I'm worried about him. He's never been in a relationship before and I don't want to see him get hurt."

"I would never hurt Ethan, Ben," I tell him. "I just want to make him happy. He deserves that, don't you think? He has never let himself have a life of his own. He deserves it. I want to be a harbor in the storm for him. I don't want to make his life harder than it already is. He's been through enough."

"I'm not saying you would hurt him. It's him I'm worried about. He's been acting so touchy lately. Everyone can see something is bothering him."

I take a deep breath. "He says he doesn't know how to do relationships because he doesn't want it to turn bad. He told me he never let himself get involved with anyone because he thought he always had to take care of you. He knows you're old enough to take care of yourself. He just doesn't know how to break out of the pattern that started when you two were little. I suppose he's nervous because this is the first time he's ever let himself have something for himself. He doesn't want to mess it up."

He lowers his eyes and sighs. "You're right. I never thought of that before, but it makes sense. He's always been protective. It is time for him to find some happiness for himself." He looks up and meets my gaze. "I really hope you can give him that. I hope you don't hold it against me the way I acted at the beginning. I would never try to come between you and Ethan."

"Of course not. I just hope you understand that I never saw you in that way."

He bursts into one of his beaming smiles. "Yeah. You made that very clear from the beginning. I was the one who was stupid for not paying attention. I'm sorry. I won't step out of line again."

I'm just about to reassure him again when Ethan comes downstairs. Ben makes himself scarce so Ethan doesn't see his brother talking to me.

I hope this doesn't turn into an awkward situation where Ben and I can't even have a civil conversation without it raising Ethan's hackles.

I say my last goodbyes to the Crenshaws and Ethan drives me home in his truck.

He walks me to the door and kisses me there for a long time, but I already feel him pulling away to leave. "Are you sure you don't want to come in?" I ask.

"I would love to, but I do need to get some sleep tonight. You might have the weekend off, but I have to work tomorrow. I've been running on fumes for too long already. I need to catch up."

I put my arms around him. "I'll miss you."

"I'll miss you, too." He buries his face in my neck. "I don't know how I'll be able to stand it without you."

I take advantage of that moment to bite his ear very gently. "I'm sure you'll be too exhausted to think about it too much."

He pulls away and kisses me to cover up the fact that he's smiling. "I'll see you soon. Behave yourself."

I blush at him. "What does that mean?"

He shakes his head in mock disappointment and heads back to his truck. "Text me....but not tonight."

I stand on the porch and watch him drive off. I can look forward to a long, lonely night full of smoking hot fantasies about him.

Chapter 22: Ivy

I wake up in the morning and spend the day cleaning my apartment. I have neglected it since I've been spending all this time with Ethan.

I change the sheets on the bed, clean the bathrooms, and clean the kitchen. I run a few errands in town and wind up back at my apartment Saturday night with nothing to do.

I haven't heard from Ethan all day, but he's probably still out at work.

I don't expect to hear from him tonight, either. He probably wants to catch up on sleep tonight after all these late nights we've been pulling.

He's the one who keeps driving back and forth between Turning Point Ranch and Coeur d'Alene while I stay home asleep in my own bed.

This whole business is coming to a head. We either need to take the next step or spend less time together for the sake of our own health—or at least Ethan's health.

I find myself drifting off into fantasies about him. I shouldn't be getting this obsessed over a man I'm barely involved with.

I can't help remembering him above me, under me, behind me, and on top of me—and every other way he's been around me.

His body drives me wild. I want his hands on me right now, but he isn't here. I don't even know when I'll see him again.

I settle onto the couch for an evening of quiet entertainment when my front door explodes off its hinges without warning.

I shoot to my feet half-expecting to see Carl coming back from the dead.

Ethan storms in instead. I've never seen him so furious—not since he shot those guys at the grocery store.

"What the hell is the matter with you?!" he thunders. "I told you not to tell anyone about me! You said you wouldn't, but that was a lie! Then you turned around and told Ben when I specifically told you not to!"

I gape at him with my mouth open. "What are you talking about?! I never told Ben anything! I would never tell anyone about that!"

"Then why did he say you did?!" he counters. "He says you told him my secret!"

My jaw drops. "I never told him, Ethan! I would never tell anyone, especially not Ben! I swear to you..."

"DON'T YOU DARE LIE TO ME!" I might have felt afraid of him if I didn't hear his voice break right then. "He told me point blank that you told him my secret and he says it's okay! You told him last night, didn't you?"

I scramble to remember my conversation with Ben in the living room.

"I talked to him while you were upstairs, but I never told him that! I'm telling the truth, Ethan! I swear it on my mother's grave! I never told anyone!"

He throws up his hands and paces away from me shaking his head, but at least he doesn't leave.

I watch him for a minute. He storms back and forth across the apartment seething in turmoil—but he isn't angry. He's yelling a lot, but he isn't angry.

It hits me in that moment. He's scared. He's petrified of anyone finding out the truth.

I take a deep breath. "What exactly did he say?"

"I just told you," he snaps over his shoulder. "He said he knows what's bothering me and it's okay."

"But....that could mean....." The puzzle pieces click. "Oh," I mumble. "I understand now."

"What are you talking about?!" he barks. "What could he possibly mean besides that?"

I brace myself to take the bull by the horns—except that Ethan is not a bull. He's a hurt, scared, wounded little boy trapped in a man's body.

I walk over to that side of the living room, but he won't come near me. He keeps pacing back and forth in front of me.

Every nerve in his big body stretches to the breaking point. He'll blow up if I try to get close to him.

"Listen to me, Ethan," I tell him. "He came up to me while you were upstairs. He apologized for being rude to me when we first met and he said he was worried about you because you've never gotten involved with anyone—not seriously—and he doesn't want to see you get hurt. He said he can see something is bothering you and he didn't know what it was."

He snorts at me over his shoulder. At least he's listening.

"I told him what you told me about always feeling like you have to take care of him. I told you never let yourself get involved with anyone because you always felt like you had to be responsible for him. I said you were worried about getting involved with me because you didn't know how to do relationships and you didn't want to mess it up. That's all I said. I swear it. I never told him about your parents. I would never betray your confidence like that. If Ben found out, he didn't hear it from me."

He barely looks at me. "This is too much. I can't trust you."

Now it's my turn to hold up my hands. "I'm sorry you feel that way, but that's your decision, not mine. You need to understand that you're not trusting me because you're making a choice not to. It isn't because I betrayed your confidence. I didn't. I wouldn't. I want you to trust me, but if you decide not to, there's nothing I can do to make you do it ."

"No, you don't understand." He turns around and confronts me for the first time. "*I* can't trust you. It isn't you. There's something wrong with me—and now this information is out there in the world just waiting to blow. No one has ever known before—and now I can't deal with one person knowing."

I try to understand what he's saying. "So.....you believe me? You believe I didn't tell Ben?"

He throws up his hands again and lets them slap down on his thighs. "I don't know how to deal with this."

"Why don't you ask him what exactly he meant?"

He faces the other way shaking his head. I don't even know what's going through his head right now, but if he doesn't trust me, then there is no way our relationship can survive.

He looks up and barely makes eye contact. "I gotta go," he mumbles. "I gotta straighten this out on my own before I do anything else."

He walks out, and a minute later, his truck drives past my duplex.

I don't try to stop him. Maybe he's too damaged for this. Maybe we're both better off apart.

I turn back to the couch, but I don't fantasize about Ethan anymore. If I never see him again, if this all comes to a crashing halt right now—maybe it's for the best.

I turn my attention to other things and go back to work on Monday morning. My life makes so much more sense when I don't have to worry about any of that drama.

I head for my office and find a bunch of emails from my supervisors. The Police Department had a data security breach over the weekend. The department's IT people think a power surge or temporary outage caused the breach.

I have to go over there and spend hours dealing with the breach. The department's IT team works in tandem with the power company's IT and data recovery team to restore the system and recover the lost data.

I get all mixed up in the middle of it. I stay at the Police Department for the rest of the day working alongside technicians from both the department and the power company.

I'm sitting at the computer rifling through a whole bunch of old power supply data when a stream of Police Department files floods my computer.

One file after another pops up on my screen. They're all old criminal cases for decades ago.

I don't know any of the people involved. Most of them are already dead, either as the suspects or the victims.

"Hey!" I call over my shoulder. "Something must have got crossed in the system. Police Department files are showing up on power company databases."

One of the Police Department guys comes over and glances at my screen. "Don't close any of the windows until we figure out how to transfer them across to the other system. Just leave them all up."

"There are hundreds of them—maybe even thousands of them," I tell him.

"All the more reason to keep them live until we can restore them to our system. Just sit tight. We're working on it."

I stare as one face after another flashes in front of my eyes. Each of these people is either the victim of a crime, the perpetrator, or a suspect.

The files stop popping up before the Police Department technicians are ready to do something. I probably shouldn't, but I wind up reading the first case file. It's right there in front of me. I can't shut it off.

The case is a grizzly murder of a drug-addicted prostitute in a Coeur d'Alene alley. She was beaten to death and then stabbed all over her body.

She had so many stab wounds in so many unlikely places that the Medical Examiner concluded the murder couldn't have been accidental or impulsive. She was even stabbed in the vagina and under each armpit. It had to be pre-meditated.

I don't want to read that, so I click to another case file. I'm hoping for something a little less nightmare-inducing.

I stare in blank disbelief when I pull up a report from the grocery store assault where Ethan shot those robbers.

The Police took statements from all the Crenshaws as well as all the customers, including me.

The Police also took Ethan's fingerprints and matched them to the automatic rifle that killed all those guys.

My heart stops when I see the fingerprint record hyperlinked to another criminal record.

Now I know I'm doing something wrong, but I have to find out. I'm too deep in this to back down now.

I click the link and a different case file opens—one that was already open on my desktop.

The technician startles me out of my wits by yelling across the room. "All right! We're ready! We have your machine synched with the Police Department database. All you have to do is save the files to the correct folder."

He comes toward me. I click away to a different case file and wind up back on the stabbing in the alley.

The technician comes back to my machine, clicks, *Save As,* and enters the folder designation where he wants me to save these files.

"Just click each one and save it to the same folder," he tells me. "I'll monitor from over here to make sure they're coming through."

I save that file. I have to wait a few seconds before it saves and I can start the process on the next file.

I take advantage of those few precious moments to maneuver the second case file onto my screen. Goosebumps erupt on my arms when I read it.

Ethan's fingerprints on the robber's automatic rifle connect back to fingerprint evidence from his parents' murder. Apparently, four-year-old Ethan didn't wipe the gun as well as he thought he did.

The Crime Scene people also identified Jax Ingram's couch-side handgun as the murder weapon that killed both Jax and Trisha.

Trisha's fingerprints were found on the knife lying right inside baby Ben's crib. The knife was found lying right next to the baby.

The Police file doesn't say a single word about any intruder, robber, or mystery shooter.

The Police file specifically identifies Ethan as the shooter and concludes that the case was both self-defense and defense of his baby brother.

The case is listed as closed. The Police aren't looking for the killer anymore because they already know who the killer was.

I get so engrossed in reading this that I forget to save the files.

"Hey!" the technician calls out. "Is something wrong? The files aren't coming through anymore."

I jump out of my skin. "Oh! Sorry! I got distracted."

I save and close the file on the Ingrams' murder. Then I save and close the file on the grocery store robbery and all the other files on my machine.

I don't finish until the end of the day, but I can't concentrate on work. I have to tell Ethan about this. I can't let him live another day with the guilt and fear that someone will find out the truth.

Chapter 23: Ethan

I stand outside the Turning Point Ranch house and stare up at the porch. I should feel relief and comfort coming back here, but I can't settle down.

I don't want to go in there. I don't want to face Ben, but I have to know the truth. I have to know if Ivy told him about me.

I can't stand the thought of anyone knowing. It's bad enough that Ivy knows—and now....if she betrayed me.....

I swallow down the sting of bile in my throat. Thinking about all of this makes me want to puke.

I've kept it buried all these years. Now it's all out in the open for the world to see.

I can't live with this. I can't live with myself—but I have to.

I might spend the next thirty years just learning how to live with it. Christ knows I never learned how to live with it in the first thirty years of my life.

I've been running and hiding from it. I can't run anymore. I have to face it, but it terrifies the shit out of me. It terrifies me more than anything else I've ever dealt with in my life.

The boys come out of the barn just then. They've just put their horses away from the day. Now it's time for all of us to go inside and shower and change our clothes for dinner. I can't face that—not with this hanging over my head.

I follow the boys inside. They all give me strange looks. They can see I'm agitated about something, but I don't interact with any of them.

I pretend to go to the kitchen while they go upstairs. I follow them a few minutes later and veer off to Ben's room.

The door stands open while he takes off his hat and shirt. He stands there in his jeans. He's as tall as I am, but not as bulky in the shoulders.

Looking at him hurts. He resembles our mother. I will never be able to forget what she looked like because his face reminds me of her every single day.

His eyebrows shoot up when he sees me walk in. "What's up?" he asks.

"I need to talk to you." I have to grit my teeth to hold myself under control.

"Okay." He sits down on the bed. "About what?"

"About Ivy," I snarl. "I need to know exactly what she told you—when you asked her about what was bothering me."

"So....you admit something is bothering you...."

"Just......" I have to stop myself from attacking him—my own brother. "Just...tell me what she said—exactly—word for word."

"First she assured me that she would never hurt you. She said she wants to make you happy and...." He has to think about it. "She said she wanted to be a harbor in a storm for you and make your life easier and that you had been through enough and that you deserved that."

"Anything else?" I snarl. "What else did she say? Just spit it out."

"She said you never let yourself get involved with anyone because you felt you had to take care of me." He looks up and his eyes glisten with tears. "Is that true? Is that why you've been alone all these years—because of me."

I can't look at him. "What else did she say?"

"That's all. She said you didn't think you knew how to have relationships and you didn't want to mess it up. That's all she said." He chokes on buried anguish and his lips tremble. "Don't be unhappy because of me. Don't let that be the reason. I couldn't live with that."

I can't deal with him. I should comfort him, but those words stab me in the guts. She was telling the truth. He doesn't know. She didn't tell him.

I'm the asshole for doubting her. I'm the asshole for barging into her apartment and accusing her of betraying me when she didn't.

Now I have to face her. She'll probably dump me because I'm too messed up to be in the same room with a woman like her.

I just have to front up to her, tell her I made a mistake, and take the consequences. I have to be a man about it even if it means I spend the rest of my life alone.

She'll find a great guy and ride off into the sunset. She deserves that. She sure as hell won't get it from me.

Ben comes up behind me. "I....I love you, man." He raises his hand, but he hesitates to put it on my shoulder. That's me. My own brother hesitates to touch me.

"I had this amazing life because of you—because you always protected me." His voice shakes with buried sobs. "Even at the grocery store......you saved all those people because of me.....I can only be the person the old man wants me to be because of you. Don't let me be the reason you're unhappy. I can't face that. I just....I love you. I don't know how else to say it."

I can't turn around. I can barely make myself heard when I rasp out, "You aren't the reason."

"She's a great girl," he tells me. "I'm happy for you. You deserve her so much more than I do. Don't let this slip away. I want to see you happy."

I love this boy more than anything. I would throw myself in front of a gun for him—and he doesn't even know that I already lost her. I won't be happy—but not because of him.

I don't deserve her. Any man would deserve her more than I do.

I can't stay in this room any longer, but I can't leave without giving him some acknowledgment.

I turn around and hug him. His presence makes me want to cry—not for us but for her—for the damage I did to her life.

The best thing I can do is to tactfully step out of it and make room for her to find someone better. That's the only thing left for me to do.

I pat Ben on the cheek and get out of his room. I have a long drive down to Coeur d'Alene and it's already almost dinner time.

I go down to the living room on my way out of the house. I can't walk out on my mother again.

She's too busy taking the corned beef out of the pot. She barely glances at me. "Hey, baby. How's it going?"

"It's fine, Mama. I gotta go to town and see Ivy. I probably won't be around for dinner, but I'll be back later tonight."

She smiles at me, puts the corned beef on a cutting board, throws off her oven mitts, and kisses me on the cheek. "Okay, sweetheart. I'm really happy you found her. Drive safely and call me if you need anything."

Dead calm settles over me on the way down the highway. I already know what will happen when I get to Ivy's apartment. She'll dump me and I'll accept it.

Then I'll have to drive home and tell the family it's over. They don't need to know the real reason why.

She kept my secret. She'll continue to keep it. She has no reason not t o.

She'll probably never have any other dealings with my family. She definitely won't have any dealings about that.

I pull up in front of her duplex and take a deep breath before I can bring myself to go in there.

This is the end of any chance I ever had to be happy. I had a great girl. I had the possibility of a great future. Now all of that is gone.

I stop outside her door and raise my hand to knock. I know better than to just walk in. I'm not welcome here anymore.

She yanks the door open before I have a chance to knock. She grabs me by the wrist and tows me inside. "Get in here!" she exclaims and shuts the door behind me.

I stare at her. "What are you doing?"

She bursts out in insane laughter. "You won't believe it, Ethan! I just found out the most amazing news!"

I square my shoulders to take the hit. "I know you didn't tell Ben about me. I'm ashamed of myself for confronting you the way I did. I know I messed up. I understand if you don't want to see me anymor e....."

"Forget all that!" she blurts out. "None of that matters!"

She won't stop grinning at me. Why is she so bubbly all of a sudden?

"Just listen to me for a second, will you?" she pants. "I was at work today. The Police Department had a data breach that crossed the system with the power company—so I accidentally saw a whole bunch of Police case files—including the case file from the grocery store shooting."

I frown at her. "What does that have to do with anything?"

She holds up her hands to silence me, but she bursts out in giggles before she can bring herself to go on.

"The Police fingerprinted you—on the gun you used to kill the robbers."

"Yeah? So?"

"The fingerprints link back to your parents' shooting. You didn't wipe the prints, Ethan. The Police lifted your prints from the gun and matched your father's gun to both shootings. The Police already know you shot your parents and they found your mother's prints on the knife in Ben's crib. The case is ruled as self-defense. Everyone already knows, Ethan. You don't have to hide from this anymore. Even Tom and Camille probably already found out. Your parents must have known all these years and never said anything because they wanted you to start a new life."

I stare at her. My brain doesn't want to register what she's telling me.

This isn't happening. All this time.....all these years spent worrying....

My mind flashes to my parents. Of course they must have known. The social workers who placed Ben and me with the Crenshaws would have told my parents everything—including the outcome of the case.

My parents are the ones who have been keeping this charade going. They're the ones who keep telling everyone year after year that my parents died in a break-in.

I can't cope with this.....and then, for no reason I can think of, I start laughing. Ivy is right. I don't have to worry about it anymore. Everyone already knows—everyone who matters.

Ben doesn't know and he doesn't need to know.

The Police know. They're the ones who ruled the killing as self-defense.

Ivy has been telling me this all along, but I didn't believe her. I have to believe the Police.

The overwhelming relief almost makes me break down crying, but it comes out as laughter instead. It's over. The nightmare I've been living since I was four years old—it's all over.

Ivy starts laughing, too. Her eyes twinkle with so much mischief and happiness. Of course she understands. Of course she understood the minute she saw the connection in the case file.

She grabs my hand. I can't keep away from her. I snatch her off the floor in a huge hug, but I can't stop laughing in pure relief. This changes everything.

She squeals when I spin her around. She feels wonderful in my arms. I can love her. I can build a life with her. I don't have to run from this anymore.

I put her down and wind up staggering backward as a wave of vertigo hits me. I have trouble standing up with all the emotions raging through me right now.

She laughs at me and tugs my hand. "Come sit down before you fall over. You'll faint away like a lady in a storybook."

I can't stop laughing. She pulls me down on the couch and then stands up to go do something.

I grab her hand and pull her in to kiss her, but we both wind up toppling backward on the couch.

I'm too relieved and emotional even to start something with her. I just want to lie here and feel her next to me.

I feel my whole body shaking with some kind of energy I don't understand. I must have been holding this in so tightly all these years. Now it's coming out of me in ways I never realized.

She curls in next to me, wraps her arms around me, and lets out a blissful sigh of relief. I feel her breaking into little bursts of happy giggles.

She doesn't think twice about me accusing her of betraying me. None of that matters anymore.

God, I love this woman! What a desert my life has been without her until now!

Never again. I turn aside and lay my lips on her forehead. "Marry me," I whisper. "I never want to let you out of my sight again."

She squeezes tightly around my ribs. "Yes," she whispers. "I love you."

I have to lift her chin and stare into her eyes as I kiss her. I can't even use my tongue. I kiss her lightly on the lips while I get lost in those eyes.

Chapter 25: Ethan

I sit on the edge of the bed and watch Ivy come out of the bath-room. She holds a white towel around her chest and another twists into a turban on top of her head.

She blushes and giggles when she sees me watching her. "Don't look at me like that."

"Like what?" I tease.

She walks away to her closet. "Don't you have some work to do?"

"It's already eight o'clock. I won't get back to the ranch until ten at the earliest. The boys will already be out working. They already know where I am."

She looks up. "They do?"

"I told my mama where I was going last night. I thought I would just come here, get dumped, and drive home—but apparently not."

She laughs, blushes, and turns away. "Nice try. You'll have to do better than that if you want to get rid of me."

I lean forward, grab her hand, and pull her between my knees. I trail my hands up and down her ass and thighs while I raise my face to kiss her. "I'm going to make you my wife."

"You better." She kisses me, smirks, and breaks away. "Are you going to watch me get dressed every morning?"

"I'm sure I'll get sick of it in ten or twenty years—after you've had a bunch of kids and I have a pot belly....."

She laughs again. "Stop it."

I can't stop myself from laughing along with her. I can't remember ever feeling this happy.

The relief of knowing I'm free—it's unlike anything I've ever felt.

I lean back on my arm and watch her change into her underwear. I'm only wearing my jeans so far. I still have to get dressed myself, but I'm enjoying myself too much to stop looking at her.

She squirms into her skirt and then buttons up her blouse over her bulging bra cups.

Her blouse covers her up, but I can still see the body underneath. She's all mine. I'm gonna take her home and keep her all to myself.

She keeps blushing at me over her shoulder while she slips into her heels, makes sure she has everything in her purse, and pulls on her blazer. "Aren't you going to put your shirt and boots on?" she asks me.

I guess I have no reason not to. I get the rest of the way dressed and spend way too long kissing her at the door before we leave.

"I'm going to marry you," I tell her.

She smirks again. "You've only been telling me every ten minutes since last night."

"I just want to make sure I don't leave any doubt in your mind."

She rises on her tiptoes to kiss me this time. "There isn't any. Now go home—and behave yourself."

I laugh. I can't remember laughing this much in all the rest of my life combined.

I wave to her through the windshield before we drive off in opposite directions.

I can barely contain my excitement all the way home. I don't even care that I'm missing work for the first time since I was a toddler.

I pull into the driveway and spot the boys working on the tops. I can't see from here what they're doing. It doesn't matter anymore.

I'll never work at Turning Point Ranch again. Yesterday was my last day of work—and I don't even care. Thinking that makes me mind-blowingly happy.

I turn off and drive up there. Wade glares at me when I get out of my truck. "You can't keep running off on us like this. I know you got a girl in town and everything...."

"I would like your permission to marry Ivy," I blurt out. "I'm going to take over Hollow River Hill and we're going to live there. I don't like leaving you boys in the lurch, but I have to think about my future and this is it. I won't be working at Turning Point anymore. I'm moving out today. I'm going to move over there and start working the place. We can arrange a time to meet up and sign Hollow River Hill over to the family trust, but I'm going to put all my effort into the other place from now on."

Silence answers me and I'm only half done.

I turn to Ben. "We would love it if you came with us, little brother. I don't want to do this alone and the place is as much yours as it is mine. I understand if you want to stay at Turning Point. It's entirely up to you and what you think is right."

"You mean......" he chokes. "You mean....you're leaving?"

"I have to." I feel my throat tightening. "I have to take this chance. I have to make good on the legacy our parents and grandparents left for us. Once we put the ranch into the family trust, all of that effort will go toward enriching the family. That's the best I can do—and I have to do it for Ivy and our future."

"But....." Ben casts a desperate glance at the men around him. "I couldn't leave Turning Point—not now. The boys need me. They need both of us."

"I'm sorry about that. I don't like leaving any more than you do, but I have to. I can't sacrifice my chance for anything—and I have to do right by Ivy and the family we're going to have."

"Of course you do." Wade steps forward, hugs me, and grips my shoulders when he holds me at arm's length. "I'm happy for you. You deserve this. You found the right woman for you."

My brothers come forward and congratulate me one after the other, but most of them have tears in their eyes.

Ben doesn't come. He stands in the back staring at me in despair.

I get through the whole group and stop in front of him. His features spasm all over the place and a tear streaks down his cheek. "Don't leave, Ethan!" he husks. "You can't leave me!"

I pull him into my arms and hug him tighter than tight. "I'll never leave you, boy—not ever. I'll see you all the time—and maybe you'll come to live with us one of these days."

I push him back, but seeing him so upset breaks something for me. I have to leave even if it means hurting him.

I don't want to leave him, either. He's all I've ever had—all except the Crenshaws.

One thought keeps me going. He might need Hollow River Hill Ranch, too, one of these days. I have to keep the ranch for him as much as for myself and Ivy.

The ranch is his. He might get married and decide to come help me on the ranch—or something might happen to me.

I want it to be as good as it can be when that day comes. I want him to step into it knowing I did my absolute best—for him, for the family, for Ivy, for our children—and for the next generation of Crenshaws coming behind us.

I break away from him and leave him standing there wiping tears off his cheeks. I love him with all my heart, but I know what I have to do.

I get in my truck, wave to the boys once, and drive off. The other boys surround Ben, hug him, and pat him on the back before they all go back to work.

I drive down to the house. Now I have to deal with Mama and the girls.

I walk in to find them all in one place. This is awfully coincidental considering the circumstances.

My mom shoots off the couch. "Where were you?! I was worried! You said you would be home last night!"

"I told you, Mama. I was at Ivy's house." I pull her back down on the couch and sit next to her. "Ivy and I are getting married, Mama. I just got Wade's approval."

She bounces off the couch clapping her hands. "This is wonderful! Congratulations!" She lunges for me and tackles me in a hug. "I'm so happy for you! This is going to be so great! Did you set a date yet? Can I call her and start making all the plans? When are you going to bring her over for dinner again?"

"Calm down, Mama," I tell her. "I need to talk to you about something. It's important."

"Weddings are important! Yee! I'm so happy!"

"Mama....I'm moving out of the house," I murmur. "I'm moving over to Hollow River Hill. Ivy and I are going to live there. I'm moving over there today to start cleaning the place up and working the ranch."

She blinks as the smile evaporates off her face. "You're....you're leaving? But.....what about Ben?"

I find it hard not to look away. "I invited him to come with us. He doesn't know what he's going to do. I suppose he'll stay at Turning Point for now until he makes up his mind."

"How did he take it?" Ava asks from the other side of the room.

I try to shake it off. "He's upset about it, naturally, but I have to do this. I have to make good on my family's inheritance."

My mom leans forward and squeezes my hand. "Of course you do, sweetheart. Of course we all understand you have to do this. It would be stupid of you to squander this inheritance—especially when you have a wife and your own family to think of." She struggles to smile at me with tears brimming in her eyes. "I'm so happy for you. Just remember where you came from, okay? Don't forget where everyone loves you."

"Thanks, Mama." I hug her, and once I start, I can't let go.

She must have known about me all along—and she didn't care. She and the old man took me even knowing what I did. They loved me the same way even knowing.

Painful love for both of them cracks my heart in half. I had two parents straight out of Heaven and the good news is that I always will. I'll always hold these people in my heart.

These are the parents that I will become. I won't become an insane, murderous, abusive psychopath.

I have the most perfect models of what my life and my future family will be. All I have to do is follow that. I won't be able to go wrong.

The girls congratulate me, too, but none of them will stop crying. They don't want to see me go even if it means my happiness.

I finally get out of there and go up to my room. It isn't my room anymore. I'll never sleep here again.

I pull my duffel bag out of the closet and start packing my work clothes into it. I can come back for my nice clothes later.

I take what I need out of the bathroom and go through the same process in reverse to get out of the house.

I get into my truck and drive away—into the future waiting for me right on the other side of those hills.

Chapter 26: Ivy

I open my apartment door and find Ethan standing on the front step. His eyes light up when he sees me. "Are you ready for this?" he asks.

"No," I reply.

He bursts out in laughter and blushes. He laughs so easily now.

His whole being glows with so much excitement about our future together. He's a completely different person than he was when I first met him.

He steps inside the apartment, gives me one kiss, and looks around until he spots my suitcases sitting by the door.

"Let's get out of here," he tells me. "Once you see it, you'll like it."

"What if I hate it?"

He smirks at me. "I'll be there. I'll distract you from everything you hate."

I make a face, but we're both too happy to care. He grabs two of my suitcases and I grab the other.

He carries those two out to his truck. I wheel mine. He puts all three of them into the truck bed. Then he and I go back and forth to the apartment and bring out all the boxes containing my possessions.

We load up the truck and he opens the passenger door so I can get in.

We both keep shooting grins at each other on our way up the highway. We hold hands and stroke our fingers over each other's knuckles.

This is right. I don't know what I'll find on the other end, but it's right. I know that for certain now.

Neither of us talks on the way up there. He turns into the driveway at Hollow River Hill Ranch.

I came out here to assess the ranch's power needs, but I never got to see inside the ranch house. No one has lived here for years.

Ben and Ethan have had a few more meetings with Bernard Kershaw to finalize the handover of Josiah Montague's estate. Bernard says the last few leaseholders only used the land around the Hollow River Hill ranch house. The leaseholders didn't live there.

Ethan has been living in the house and working the land for a week to clean the place up, but he says it needs a lot of work. The whole place could be falling down for all I know.

We'll just have to fix it up. If that's the worst problem we face together, we'll be getting off easy.

The driveway curves around a few rolling hills. The land around here looks as good as Turning Point—as good as Eastwood and Iron Mountain.

It's nice to know my neighbors on both sides are Ethan's brothers and their wives. Family will never be far away—and Turning Point is right down the road.

Ethan and I will go over there all the time for family dinners and events. I have no doubt about that.

I'm excited about getting to work and making Hollow River Hill our own. I can't wait to start living here in our own house. No more rentals for me.

Ethan drives around the last hill and we see the ranch house. It's an old-fashioned clapboard farmhouse like the houses at Eastwood and Iron Mountain. This isn't a modern, sprawling mansion like the Turning Point Ranch house.

Ethan parks, opens my door for me, and takes out my suitcases. He carries two of them, but the third one is too heavy for me to carry over the uneven ground. That suitcase was made to wheel along paved sidewalks, not over dirt clods and patches of scrubby grass.

He sets the suitcases on the porch and throws open the front door for me. "Go ahead inside and explore around. Make a list of everything you hate. I'll bring in your stuff and we can compare notes when you finish."

He smiles at me one more time and goes back to his truck. I slip inside.

Hardwood floors extend down the long hallway to the backdoor leaving the house at the far end.

A huge, carved wooden staircase with an ornate, polished banister rises to the second story.

A magnificent crystal chandelier hangs from the carved plaster ceiling high above the front hall. Swooping angels and decorative borders surround the chandelier.

They give the whole house a cathedral atmosphere like an old castle transported to the middle of Idaho.

A large living room branches off the front hall to the right. A carved timber arch separates the living room from a spacious dining room with a massive table surrounded by ten antique chairs.

I stop in each room staring at the vintage furniture, the magnificent crown moldings over every door and window, sweeping curtains, and extravagant carpet.

There is no way Ethan could have done all of this in a week. The house must have been originally built like this—and it's still exquisite.

I follow the hall to the kitchen in the very back. It's a farmhouse style kitchen with a big table surrounded by more chairs. This is where the ranch family shares everyday meals when they aren't eating in the dining room.

All the fixtures in the kitchen are vintage, too, including the stove, the fridge, and the sink and its fixtures.

They give the kitchen a quaint, homey feel. Nothing here feels cheap, dilapidated, or falling apart.

I see the same style of décor in all the bedrooms upstairs. The big master bedroom sits at the end of the top floor landing.

A giant dark wooden four-poster bed occupies the center of the room. A curved leather vintage couch sits in front big windows looking out over the ranch.

All my tension and doubt drains out of me when I sit down on the couch. I absolutely love this house. This is my house—mine and Ethan's new home.

He comes up the stairs just then, finds me in the bedroom, and puts his arm around me when he sits down next to me.

"So what's the verdict?" he asks. "Should we burn it down and rebuild something more to your taste?"

I can't even take the joke. I lean against him and rest my head on his shoulder. "I love it. Thank you."

He kisses the top of my head, but just then, we hear truck engines outside.

I follow him outside just as the Crenshaw boys roll up followed by three loaded stock trucks.

I stand on the porch and watch Ethan and the boys signal the drivers, drive out to the pastures, and release the cattle onto the land.

The boys spend a long time signing off with the drivers, letting the trucks out so they can leave, and then going around to double-check all the water troughs, fences, and gates.

They come back over to the house to get into their own vehicles. Wade waves to me. "Hey, Ivy."

"Hi, boys," I reply. "Thank you for bringing the stock over. This place needs it."

"It's a great place." He claps Ethan on the back. "You two are going to knock this out of the park."

"Thanks, brother," Ethan murmurs.

Wade pulls him into a hug. "Don't be a stranger. We're all pulling for you."

Ethan shuts his eyes and his face crunches up in a moment of agony when he hugs Wade. The rest of the brothers come forward to shake Ethan's hand, congratulate him, and wish him all the best.

Ben hangs back until the very end. Ethan gets progressively more emotional each time he says goodbye to one of his brothers. This is it—the final break.

Ethan comes to a halt in front of his brother. Ben's features spasm all over the place and tears streak down his cheeks.

They attack each other in a brutal hug that doesn't end. Neither of them will let go—and then Ben breaks down sobbing on his brother's shoulder.

Ethan fights to control his features when he cups the back of Ben's neck and pulls him in deeper. Ethan doesn't let go.

Some of the other brothers turn away wiping their eyes. I find my eyes stinging watching Ben and Ethan together.

Ben doesn't even try to hide his anguish when they pull apart and he straightens up to face Ethan.

Ethan squeezes his brother's neck and strokes the tears off Ben's cheeks. I know exactly how that feels.

"You always have a home here," Ethan murmurs. "Never forget that."

Ben half-whimpers, half-wails out, "Yes, Sir."

"You go with the boys," Ethan tells him. "I'll see you in a few days if not before. Understand? The boys will take care of you."

Ben whimpers, "Yes, Sir."

Ethan pulls him in, kisses Ben on the forehead, and pushes him away. Ethan backs away, but Ben doesn't. The other boys break for their trucks.

Ben waits until the very end. He stands there sobbing his eyes out. I can't help but shed tears at the sight of him.

I wish like anything he was coming here to live with us. I can't stand seeing him and Ethan separate.

This will be the first time they have ever lived apart. I don't think any of the brothers realized just how hard it would be for both of them when Ethan moved away.

He moved less than a mile down the road. They'll work together almost every day, but it still tears my heart out.

The boys fire up their engines. Two trucks drive off. Nathan stays behind alone to take Ben back to Turning Point.

Ethan points at him. "Go on, Ben. Go with Nathan."

Ben turns away, walks back to Nathan's truck, gets into the passenger seat, and bows his head sobbing like a little boy. Nathan waves to Ethan and Ethan raises his hand once before Nathan drives off.

Ethan stands there for a long time watching the line of trucks disappear. I can't see from here if Ethan is crying, too.

I can't keep away from him. If he isn't crying on the outside, he must be crying on the inside.

I walk up behind him, slip my arms around his waist, and hug him. I would do anything to give him Ben back, but that isn't going to happen—not now.

Ethan turns around sooner than I expect. He twists backward in my arms and folds me in his big, warm embrace. We hold onto each other for dear life.

We're all alone now. Whatever happens on this ranch will be up to us. It's our job to make it work no matter what. The whole Crenshaw clan is counting on us.

Ethan sacrificed a lot to come and work here. The boys need him at Turning Point.

He is going to have to make Hollow River Hill Ranch a success in its own right to justify taking himself away from Turning Point.

He straightens up sooner than I expect. He does his best to smile at me, but I can't help but see plenty of sadness in that smile.

"Let's get this party started," he tells me. "You go inside and start being a ranch housewife. Your man has work to do."

Chapter 27: Ethan

I come into the house from working on the ranch—my ranch. Hollow River Hill is my place now.

I find myself stopping every now and then just to look around. I never understood before why Gabe and Jake both moved away to start their own operations separate from Turning Point.

Now I get it. This is my place—mine, Ivy's, and Ben's.

Separating from him is the hardest thing I've ever had to do—but he's still here. This is his ranch as much as mine.

I owe it to him to do this right—and I will.

I've never been more certain of Ivy. She fits right in here. She'll make a perfect ranch wife—and she loves the house—our house.

I walk in and hear her banging around in the kitchen. I go in there, but I leave immediately when I see her working between the stove, the fridge, and the counters.

She looks like she found the groceries I brought in. She has a bunch of cutting boards, knives, and vegetables laid out on the counters. Three frying pans and a pot of boiling water simmer on the stove.

I go upstairs, take a shower, and put on clean clothes for dinner. I go down to the kitchen, kiss her, and sit down at the kitchen table to watch.

"So....wife...." I begin.

She shoots me a smirk over her shoulder. "We aren't married yet, remember?"

"That's just a technicality. Did you know that in some African cultures, a couple doesn't have to do anything to get married? They just go home to the same house together and that's it. They're married."

"I think you just made that up to suit your own purposes," she replies over her shoulder.

"So what if I did?"

She laughs. "I hope you like Indian food because that's what we're eating tonight."

"I love Indian food. Thank you."

"I have some big shoes to fill following in your mama's footsteps. I'm going to have to step up my game to keep you suitably impressed."

"I'm already impressed," I tell her.

She laughs again, but she doesn't answer. She's too busy.

She has no idea how impressed I am with everything she does. She's so enthusiastic about all of this. Her attitude and energy inspire me to work harder.

"How are the stove and fridge working out for you?" I ask.

She doesn't turn around. "What do you mean?"

"We could upgrade them to something more modern."

"No way!" she exclaims and crosses the kitchen to pull something out of the fridge. "They're cute! They're sweet! They have personality."

"But how well do they work?"

She frowns at me before she goes back to cutting the vegetables. "They work just fine. Haven't you been making food for yourself in here all week? Don't you already know?"

"I'm not the one who is going to be slaving over a hot stove in here. You are. I don't want you to struggle to make this work. If you want to change them, we can. We can use the money my grandfather left us."

"That isn't necessary. They work fine the way they are. They work just as well as anything I had at that duplex. Don't waste money on things we don't need. Save the money in case another disaster strikes and we need to use the money for something essential."

I shrug even though she isn't looking at me. "You're right. Good thinking."

She stops what she's doing, wipes her hands on a towel, comes over to me, and sits down sideways on my lap.

She wraps her arms around my neck and kisses me. "I really appreciate you thinking of me. If something doesn't work, I'll tell you—but right now, I'm loving the house the way it is. I don't want to change anything."

"Far be it for me to deny my new bride anything she wants."

She laughs again, kisses me, and goes straight back to work.

"I have a question," she goes on over her shoulder.

"Go ahead."

"How soon do you want to start having kids?"

My head shoots up. "What?"

"How soon do you....?"

"I heard you. Why do you ask that?"

She leans her hip against the kitchen counter, turns to face me, and stirs one of her sizzling frying pans while we talk. "I ask because I'm on a birth control shot that stops me from getting pregnant for six months at a time. I won't be able to get pregnant for another three months—and then if you wanted to delay, I would need to get another one to cover the next six months. That's why I ask. You never asked me about it before—so I'm telling you now. I thought we ought to talk about it before we got married." She makes a face. "We probably should have talked about it before we moved in together, but I figured we both already wanted kids. It was just a question of when—which is why I'm bringing it up now."

I gulp. "Um....so you and Trey were planning to wait?"

She winces and covers it up by taking the pan off the stove. "I never told Trey I got the shot. He started acting more and more unstable the longer we were married. I was on the pill when we met. We decided I would stay on it until we were ready to start having kids. Then he started acting weird—getting really jealous and controlling for no reason. He threatened me a few times before the actual gun incident. It was after his behavior changed that he pressured me to go off the pill so we could get pregnant. I realized it was a terrible idea, but I couldn't let him see that I was still on birth control. I went off the pill and got the shot." She looks up and meets my eyes. "I hope that doesn't make you think any less of me."

I don't know what to say, so I just mumble, "No, it doesn't make me think any less of you."

"I wasn't sure if he was just going through something—or maybe we could work it out—or maybe I could somehow be good enough to convince him that I wasn't doing anything to betray him. I told myself I could just play along until he calmed down and then I could go off the shot when I thought it was safe to bring a child into the situation. Then, after a while, he deteriorated and I started thinking about actually running away from him. I was planning to do it when the whole gun incident happened."

"Did he find out you planned to run away?"

"No, something else triggered it. I got a phone call from my cousin who was deployed overseas in the military. I was on the phone with him for five hours and Trey found out. That's why he attacked me. He saw the call and realized that I was talking to another guy. Trey didn't know who the other guy was, so he completely flipped out. Anyway, that's why I kept up with the shot—because I thought, if I had to run for it, I didn't want to be pregnant or have a baby while I was doing it "

I don't answer. We've never talked about her marriage in this much detail.

I really need to talk to Anna about this—and Ivy probably needs to talk to Anna about this. Anna's husband wasn't abusive, but we still need support for this.

Ivy needs to understand that other women in the family can relate to what she's going through—or what she has been through. I wish I had thought of this before.

I should ask Jake. Fortunately, he lives right next door. If Ivy needs anything, I can just send her over there to see Anna.

Ivy notices my silence. She turns around and studies me. "So what do you want to do about the shot? Do you want me to stay on it or go off it?"

My mind goes into a tailspin thinking of all the possibilities. She'll be fertile in three months. She could get pregnant as soon as that. Am I really ready for that? Are either of us really ready for that?

"Ethan?" she asks. "Say something. You're scaring me."

I look up at her and hold out my hand. "Come here, baby."

I pull her into my lap, kiss her, and rock her in my arms before I pull back enough to look deep into her eyes. I get lost in the vast depths of her soul.

"You never have to worry about me, baby," I tell her. "Not ever. If I have something on my mind, you never have to worry that I'm doubting you or us. It's just a lot to think about, you know."

"I know." Something pops on the stove. She gets off my lap, goes over there, and starts whizzing around the kitchen again.

She takes everything off the fire, drains the pot of boiling water into the sink, mixes some of the pans' contents together with each other, and starts setting the table in front of me.

She blushes when she puts the plate and cutlery in front of me. "Am I being domestic enough for you?"

"All you need is a French maid outfit and you'll be perfect."

She laughs and goes back to the kitchen. She serves fragrant rice, stir-fried beef and veggie curry, and places a tall glass of iced tea next to my elbow.

I should thank her for this, but those words don't even begin to express how I feel about her.

I find myself studying her across the table. My wife.

"Why don't we decide each time you're scheduled to get the next shot?" I tell her. "We'll discuss this when your next shot comes around. Then we'll decide whether to extend it for another six months."

"I don't want to wait too long," she tells me. "I'm not getting any younger, you know."

"I know."

"I also don't want to get into a cycle where we keep delaying and delaying and delaying while we wait for the most perfect circumstances. I would rather have the kids sooner and just deal with whatever comes."

I chew my curry and look up at her. How the hell did I get so lucky as to marry this woman? It's true we aren't technically married yet, but we might as well be if we're having this conversation.

She wants to dive in, have kids, and take what comes.

She studies me right back. "What are you thinking?" she asks.

"I'm thinking you're smarter than I am and you're right. Let's go ahead and skip the next shot. You can go off it and we'll take what comes."

She freezes and her eyes fall out of their sockets. "Really?"

"Isn't that what you just said?"

"Yeah, but....not now!! I didn't mean right now!"

"Why not right now? We're getting married in three weeks. That leaves two more months of wild, passionate, animal sex before we have to think about you getting pregnant."

She doesn't take the joke. "You mean..... you want to do it *now?*"

I shrug. "A lot of people do it with a lot less. If we don't do it now, when would we do it? What were you thinking? You said you didn't want to delay."

"I didn't mean now!" she practically yells. "We should wait at least one more cycle—six months—that's nine months from now."

I shrug again. "Okay. We can do that." I point my fork across the table at her. "But only one six-month delay. You definitely will go off it then—no questions asked. Do we agree?"

She looks down at her plate and pushes her food around. "Yes. We agree."

"What's the matter? Isn't this what you wanted?"

She nods. "It just seems so real all of a sudden."

I lean forward and grab her hand. "It's going to be wonderful. Hey! Come here!"

I pull her back into my lap and just hold her. I could take her right now, but I don't. I don't even want to.

I just want to sit here with her and feel how much I love her. My life is so much better with her in it.

Chapter 28: Ivy

I wake up with my arms around Ethan's bare chest. His ribs rise and fall with his breathing.

I barely open my eyes and clamp them shut immediately when I see where we are.

We're in the master bedroom at Hollow River Hill—in our own house, our own bedroom. We're home.

I snuggle deeper into his arms. The sky is just turning grey outside. Another day is about to dawn on the ranch.

Ethan will work out there all day by himself—because this is our place now. He's running his own ranch just like his brothers next door.

I love him so much for that. I love the life he's giving me.

I try to go back to sleep. I still have to drive down to Coeur d'Alene to work for the power company for another month. Then Ethan and I will get married and I'll pivot into a mentorship role at the company.

I'll work from home so I don't have to commute to town and back every day. My wages will help get the ranch off the ground so we don't put too much of a burden on Turning Point.

I don't want to get up for work. I want to stay in bed with Ethan all day and all night, but that isn't going to happen.

It definitely won't happen once we start having kids. Nine months. It sounds a lot shorter than it is. Nine months is nothing. Did I really agree to that?

The wild, passionate, animal sex between now and then sounds pretty good, but not as good as spending the rest of my life with Ethan and raising a family of our own.

I want that, but it still scares me. I can't think of anyone I would rather raise a family with.

Our children will be another generation of Crenshaws. If our children turn out anything like this generation of Crenshaws, I'll have nothing to complain about. Tom and Camille have every right to be proud of the way their children turned out.

I'm just about to drift off when Ethan stirs. His arms tighten around me—and his body stiffens when he feels me lying next to him.

I'm still half-asleep when he takes hold of my wrist and slides my hand down between his legs. My fingers close around his iron shaft. He's wide awake and hard as granite.

His heat rushes up my arm and squirms between my legs. He's so damn hot. He turns me on just lying here on his back.

I stroke him until his veiny flesh pulses in my hand. His hardness excites me beyond anything I've ever known.

I push myself up on my elbow, start kissing him, and throw my leg over him to straddle him.

He reacts instantly, grabs me, and sits up on the edge of the bed with my thighs still spread around his waist.

He sits me down on him with no preamble at all. His arms clamp around my body and move me up and down on his shaft to drill into me.

I try to scream, but he smothers me in a million kisses. His body electrifies my senses and I escalate faster than ever.

He devours my mouth and his shaft splits me apart. I scream into his mouth and dissolve in the heavenly feeling of losing my mind in his intoxicating power.

He keeps guiding me down on him with masterful strokes. He doesn't stop until he contracts his stomach, crushes me all the way down on his spike, and floods me with his essence.

He growls and snarls into my mouth as his muscles contract and shiver all over his body. He feels incredible like this.

He only hesitates for a second before he grumbles under his breath and starts pumping into me a second time, but right then, his alarm goes off.

He lets go of me long enough to switch it off, checks his notifications once, and collapses onto his back on the mattress with me still clinging to him chest.

I kiss him all over his face, but I'll only start spiraling my hips on him again if we stay like this.

I give him one last luscious kiss, climb off him, and go get in the shower. He's waiting for me when I get out, kisses me, laughs when we both start to get turned on again, and swats my ass before he gets into the shower after me.

I get dressed and go down to the kitchen to make him breakfast. I'm just scooping his scrambled eggs onto a plate and pouring him a cup of coffee when he comes downstairs fully dressed.

He's just in the act of sticking his hat on when I move out of the way so he can sit down at the kitchen table.

We talk a little bit about the day, but we already know what we have to do.

"Liza and Emma were planning to come over this evening and talk to me about the wedding," I tell him. "But I just got a text from Emma to say she can't make it. She has to take Tati back to the hospital."

He shakes his head over his plate. "Poor Hank. He better not try to go to work today."

"He isn't. He's going with them—so Emma asked me to ask you to check in with Wade later to see if they need another pair of hands at Turning Point."

He frowns. "That's strange. I wonder why he didn't text me himself."

"The message didn't come from him. It came from Emma. Maybe Wade doesn't want to take you away from Hollow River Hill so soon. Maybe he's too proud to ask."

"Okay. I'll check on the stock and then drive over there to see if they need anything."

I look up at him. "Are you sure you're okay with that?"

"What do you mean? Why wouldn't I be okay with it? They're my brothers."

"I'm talking about Ben. It's gonna be really hard on him if he keeps getting so upset every time he sees you."

He looks down at his food again. "I wish I could convince him to come live here. He's trying to do the right thing by staying at Turning Point when he obviously doesn't want to. He doesn't want to leave the boys short-handed."

"He wouldn't be leaving the boys short-handed if you two are always going over there to help out."

He doesn't look up. He isn't eating anymore. "I think I'll tell him to today if he gets emotional about it. I'll tell him to just come and be done with it. I'll tell him we can go help the boys every damn day if we have to as long as he and I are together."

I love how much his brother means to him, but I can't even smile when I see how sad Ethan looks about this. He obviously needs Ben as much as Ben needs him.

He puts his fork down. "I'm sorry, baby. I can't finish this."

"Don't worry about it. I'll clean up here. Come on. Let's get to work. You can go over to the ranch and see Ben now before the boys leave for the day."

We both stand up and he takes my hand to kiss me. "Thank you," he murmurs. "Thank you for being okay with Ben coming to live here."

"Of course! He's family. He's always welcome here—and you two obviously belong together. You don't have to explain that to me."

He kisses me one more time. "I love you. I'll text you later and tell you what he says."

"I love you, too. Have a good day—and make sure he knows I'm more than happy if he comes."

"I will. Have a good day at work." He kisses me one last time and turns away.

At that moment, a brilliant flash of white-blue light flashes across the kitchen windows. It's still too dark outside for that light to come from anywhere else.

A catastrophic boom cracks across the landscape outside and a massive explosion goes off right above our heads.

Ethan dives for me, tackles me to the floor next the table, grabs me in his arms, and rolls both of us under the table as the kitchen ceiling implodes and rains mountains of debris into the room to bury us under the rubble.

Chapter 29: Ivy

I huddle in Ethan's arms and hold onto him with all my might. He lays his hand on my head and hugs me against him.

What sounds like hundreds of thunderclaps crash and boom outside the house. They echo through the walls from all sides. They sound like they're all around us.

All the debris lying on top of and around the table muffles the sound. At least none of those lightning strikes sounds like they're hitting the house again.

We lie pressed against each other for a long, long time. Neither of us moves or even breathes until the noise stops.

Even then, it takes a long time before either of us loosens our grip enough to separate.

"Are you okay, baby?" Ethan murmurs.

"Yeah!" I gasp. "Thank you! You saved me again!"

He doesn't accept the compliment. He pushes me up and looks at me with huge eyes. "I don't care about the house as long as you're okay."

I kiss him in the dark. Barely any light sneaks into this little hole through all the crap out there in the kitchen.

We both turn to the mountain of rubble blocking us from getting out of here.

"This isn't good," he mutters. "We might be stuck in here. Let me see if I can call someone."

I have to squirm off him and lie on the floor at his side while he takes his phone out of his pocket. The table only gives us a few feet of space—just enough for us to lie side by side between the tabletop and the floor.

He taps on his phone screen to turn it on. He has to use his thumbprint to unlock it.

"Cell reception is down again," he mutters." We're on our own here."

"Should we wait for the reception to come back on?"

"That could take days. It took four days last time. We don't want to wait that long." He twists onto his side, faces the debris lying across the kitchen, and pushes.

He strains all his muscles, but nothing moves. Then he rolls onto his back and pushes against the tabletop. Still nothing.

He sinks back down on the floor. "Okay," he pants. "Plan B."

"What's that?" I ask.

He shoots me a grin. "I don't know. Any ideas?"

I try to look around me, but there isn't anything here to see. Fallen timbers, broken plaster, and snapped-off wooden boards block the two sides of the table where the chairs usually stand.

If the fallen ceiling is lying across the table in a mass too heavy for Ethan to lift, then the debris on the two sides of the table will be too heavy to lift, too.

I don't know what to say, but right then, Ethan shuffles on his shoulders to turn his back to the kitchen.

"Move under me, baby," he tells me. "I'm going to try to push it up with my back. Maybe I'll be able to move it then."

I lie down on the floor. He rolls up onto his arms and pushes himself onto all fours.

I stretch out underneath him and wedge my hands against the tabletop.

He strains and groans again trying to straighten his back against the tabletop from underneath, but it still won't budge.

He collapses breathing heavily. "The whole kitchen must have fallen in—which means the upstairs bedroom must have fallen on top of us, too."

"Wait, Ethan," I tell him. "I think I have an idea."

He looks up. "What is it?"

"The floor. We can't get out going up or to any of the sides. That leaves down. This house has a basement under the floor. We can break through the floorboards and get out through the basement."

He frowns at me. "How do you say we break through the floorboards? We would need a power saw to do that."

"No, we don't. Feel this. The impact cracked some of the boards. They're already broken."

I take his hand and guide them to the boards underneath where I'm lying. I felt them shift when I put my weight on them just now.

He can move at least one of the floorboards down an inch. It levers away from the broken-off end of the same board where they cracked.

"You're a genius, baby!" he murmurs.

He dives in, kisses me, and undulates his body on top of me.

That kiss builds in passion and his body tenses pressing down on me.

He breaks off my mouth and bursts into a wild, mischievous grin when he rises on top of me. He drills his pelvis between my legs.

"Do you think I could pound you hard enough to drive you into the basement?" he pants.

I claw at him trying to pull him deeper into me. His eyes spiral me out of my mind, but I can't spread my legs wide enough in this cramped space.

"You could try, but we aren't in the right position to break that board," I tell him.

He laughs and rolls off me. "Too bad. I'll just have to save that for after we get out of here."

I roll toward him, slip my hand between his legs, and squeeze his swollen package. "I'm sure you don't need to use this disaster as an excuse."

He dives in and kisses me deep and hard for a second before we both break away.

"Business first," he breathes. "Scoot over here, baby. Let me get on top of the crack."

"You better not be getting on top of any crack other than mine," I tell him.

He bursts out laughing and blushes in the shadows. "Yes, Ma'am. I'm your humble servant. Now move over so I can examine your crack."

I join in the joke while we go through a complicated maneuver of changing our positions.

I scoot across the floor to lie closer to the kitchen. He climbs on top of me to rotate over to where I was just lying.

We both burst out laughing when he puts his weight on top of me again. Then we roll apart giggling. Now we're in opposite positions on the floor.

Laughter seems like the best way to deal with this emergency. It makes us both feel better. Neither of us gets depressed or upset that we can't get out of the kitchen.

He twists onto his stomach right on top of the cracked floorboard. He rummages in his pocket, pulls out his pocketknife, props himself on his elbows, and uses his arms to try to push the board the rest of the way down into the basement.

The board only moves a few inches, but we can see the basement. We'll be able to get out from under the house. We just have to find a way to get down there.

He pops open his knife and jams the blade into the junction point at the end of the broken board. He tries to pry it up and loosen the nails, but that doesn't work, either. They're too tight and the knife isn't strong enough.

He sinks back down on his elbows and looks around. "All right. Plan C."

"Hold it, Ethan. I think I have another idea."

"I can't wait to hear it," he tells me.

"We'll both push on the board. Both of us pushing on it should be enough to force it all the way through."

"Then how do we break the other boards?" he asks. "None of them is cracked. That one section doesn't give us enough space to get out."

"Let's start with that."

Now I have to maneuver myself onto my elbows. This little cave of ours really doesn't give us enough room to both lie in that position, but we have to make it work.

We both prop our arms on top of the broken board. Ethan rears as high onto his knees as he can, jams his shoulders against the tabletop again, and we both put as much weight as we can on the broken board.

We force it down and it tears off. It falls into the basement. Now we can both look down into space under the house.

"Well, we're getting somewhere," Ethan murmurs. "Move back, baby. I'm going to try something. You might want to cover your face."

I don't know what he's going to do, but I back away as far as I can get. I flatten myself against the fallen debris so I give him as much room as possible.

He squirms and wriggles around until he maneuvers himself backward on the same spot. He stretches out with his head near my feet and his legs closer to my head.

I'm just about to ask why he went to all that trouble when he raises his foot and smashes his bootheel down into the board right next to the open gap.

He keeps pounding it again and again with all his strength until he shatters that board and the one on the opposite side of the gap.

"Good job!" I exclaim when he stops for air. "That should be plenty of room for me to get out, but no way could you fit through there."

"Forget that," he pants. "Once you get out, you can go to the barn and get me a crowbar. I'll be able to break out the rest of the floor once I don't have to worry about hitting you."

He turns himself around and we both use our arm strength to push and tear out the broken floorboards. The gap turns out to be much bigger than I realized.

"You go first, baby," he tells me.

I kiss him again. I love him more than ever because we can deal with this situation.

"You're right," I tell him. "Let's not wait another six months. I'll go off the shot in three months. Why wait?"

His head shoots up. "Are you sure? We don't have to rush into anything."

"If we can handle this, we can handle anything. Things won't be any better in nine months. Let's just do it now."

He blinks at me, too stunned to answer. Three months. That doesn't leave much time.

I kiss him again and swing my legs through the hole into the basement. I jump down onto the concrete floor and climb the stairs to the storm doors that lead outside.

The lightning storm is over. I don't see any damage, but we could be facing another power outage or any number of other problems.

I don't care because Ethan I will face them together.

I climb out, run to the barn, grab the crowbar out of his toolbox, and use a stepladder in the basement to hand the crowbar up through the hole to him.

I go back outside while he bangs and smashes a wider hole in the floor so he can get out. He meets up with me in the driveway and puts his arms around me. "I love you."

"We can handle anything together." I kiss him. "We're unstoppable."

He laughs—and then we both see the back of the house caved in. "It looks like we might be staying at Turning Point for a little longer until we can get this fixed."

"Do you want to go around and check our stock first?"

He frowns at me. "Don't you have to go to work? You'll be extra busy after this."

"I probably should." I look down at my suit. I'm covered in dirt and dust. "I can't go like this."

"Stay here," he tells me. "I don't want you going into the house. The rest of it might be unstable."

He goes into the house and I see him moving around in the master bedroom window before he comes back out carrying one of my other suits on a hangar. "You can change in the barn."

We both laugh on our way to the barn. I change right there in plain view. I don't have to hide myself from him.

He escorts me to my car and opens the driver's door for me. "Come to Turning Point after work, okay?" he tells me. "If the house is safe for us to keep living here, I'll go over to the ranch to get you. I don't want you coming here until we know for certain."

"Okay. I'll see you later. Have a good day. I love you."

I kiss him again, but I'm already late for work.

Epilogue: Ivy

I blink back tears when I look at myself in the mirror. My white wedding gown drapes to the floor and my veil hangs over my face.

I look incredible. I never looked this good when I married Trey.

Thinking about him brings tears to my eyes—not because I regret anything that happened with him. I don't even regret marrying him.

All of that brought me to this moment—this moment when I can be happy about marrying Ethan.

Grace, Liza, Emma, and Camille all sniff behind me. "Oh, sweetheart!" Camille chokes. "You look so beautiful!"

Liza's voice trembles like she's trying to keep herself under control. "Don't start crying, Ivy, or we'll all start bawling."

I can't look at myself anymore or I really will start crying. I turn around to face them, Ava, Lucy, and Anna.

All of them stand around me in Camille's bedroom. Ethan and I have been staying at Turning Point while the construction crew repairs our house at Hollow River Hill.

I've been so busy getting ready for the wedding in between working that I haven't been able to check to see how well Ben is coping with having us around.

He acts natural when Ethan and I see Ben at mealtimes. If Ben is upset about the situation, he doesn't show it.

Ethan is too busy to tell me much. He and his brothers have to work late into the night and get up in the dark hours of the morning to deal with all the damage to all four ranches.

Hollow River Hill got off the easiest of all four. We just had to move back to Turning Point. The rest of Hollow River Hill is just fine.

The other three ranches are all dealing with devastating damage and dead livestock. Ethan barely has time to wolf down his food and collapse in bed before he gets up and does it all over again.

I don't hold out much hope that things will change after the wedding. He and I will go home to our own house tonight after the reception. Then everything will go on in the same way with Ethan working his tail off to help his brothers.

At least I won't have to leave the house every day or drive all the way to Coeur d'Alene. I'll be able to save money on gas and still earn a paycheck to help the family. So that's a plus.

I can't help but get emotional when I look around the room at all these amazing women. They really are family to me—the family I never had.

They've been so great in supporting Ethan and me plus planning the whole wedding.

Every woman here treats me like I'm one of them. They don't act like I'm any different from Grace, Liza, Lucy, or Anna.

Ethan is getting married. He'll be the same as Wade, Nathan, Gabe, Jake, Nolan, and Hank. Nothing changes—and now I'm part of that.

Just then, someone knocks on the door. It's Hank. "Is Ivy ready to go?"

"I'm ready!" I call. "I'm on my way!"

The women surround me in a huge group hug. Most of them are already crying—and then little Eli starts crying. Grace has to deal with him, but I have more important things to worry about. I'm about to get married.

The women fuss around me trying to straighten my dress on my way out of the room. Hank meets me outside.

He has been unbelievably kind to me even though he's dealing with his own stuff right now. His grandmother is in hospice care down in Coeur d'Alene.

She only has a few days to live, but he's here to support me and Ethan. As soon as the wedding ends, Hank and Emma will drive straight back to town so he can spend as much time as he can with his grandmother in the short time she has left.

The rest of the family would be down there with him, but the boys have too much work to do and already too few men to do it. They're already taking the day off work so Ethan and I can get married.

Hank smiles at me when I walk out of the room. "Ready?" he asks.

I gasp for air. I'm already having difficulty breathing. "Ready!" I pant.

He holds out his arm and leads me to the stairs. I hear the women crying behind me on our way down to the living room.

My heart starts racing when I see the wedding set up on the lawn in the backyard. A bunch of guests sit in the seats on both sides of the red-carpet aisle.

Ethan stands in front of the white rose arch with the minister standing nearby. Jack stands alone behind Ethan. All the other brothers gather in the living room waiting for me to arrive.

The family divides itself into pairs. Chuck escorts his mother to her seat in the front row. Then Wade and Grace, Liza and Nathan. Ava and Nolan, Gabe and Lucy, Jake and Anna, and Hank and Emma all walk down the aisle in front of me.

The brothers break off to the groom's side. The wives all stand on the left except for Grace. She sits down next to Camille and props Eli on her lap.

Ben comes up to me from the side. The two of us are the last ones left.

His eyes swim with tears when he smiles at me. He looks unbelievably happy for the first time in a long time.

He holds out his elbow and I slip my hand into it as the bridal march starts playing over the speakers.

I turn—and see Ethan standing at the far end of the aisle. It's so fitting that Ben should be the one giving me away.

I know he's happy for us. He couldn't be happier that Ethan is finally finding the love he deserves. Ethan doesn't have to be alone anymore. No one is happier about that than Ben.

The rest of the world disappears, but I have to stand by while Ben and Ethan hug each other in a deep, close embrace. Ethan compresses his lips to hold back emotion when he clasps his brother's cheek.

Ben tears himself away and his brothers pull him into line with the rest of the groomsmen. Now it's just me and Ethan, together under the clear blue sky.

The minister starts the service and I go into a trance. Ethan and I are all alone here. We'll be alone even when we're surrounded by family.

The ceremony ends and I share a million hugs, tears, laughs, and smiles with all my new favorite people. We go through the reception getting congratulated by everyone until the time comes for me and Ethan to get into his truck and go home.

I change out of my wedding dress in Camille's room. I put on one of my business suits.

Everyone yells at me and Ethan and they throw rice at us when we run for his truck. He opens the passenger door so I can get in.

We wave from the windows. Everyone calls out to us and waves as we drive away. Ethan clasps my hand. We're together. We're married. Nothing can tear us apart.

We drive home to Hollow River Hill and we both pause when we get out and look at our house.

The kitchen has been rebuilt along with part of the upstairs bedroom that collapsed on top of us. The construction has been going on since the day after the lightning strike.

The construction crew only finished working on the house the day before yesterday. The girls have been slaving away behind my back to clean everything up before Ethan and I came home.

Ethan grabs my hand and squeezes. "Ready?" he asks.

"Ready," I tell him and we both start forward. Our whole life is waiting for us in there. All we have to do is buckle our seatbelts and meet it head-on.

<u>End of Book 7.</u>

Keep Reading

Cowboys of Turning Point Ranch Series: Book 8: Lost Love

Ben Ingram can't believe it when his high school girlfriend comes back to town all grownup, stunningly beautiful—and married. Ben and Zoe Joplin probably would have gotten married, but she went away to college and he never saw her again.

Now she's back with a whole lot of problems of her own. Her husband gets irrationally jealous when he sees her talking to Ben. Could Zoe's husband see something in their innocent conversation that Ben and Zoe don't see?

Ben has his own struggles to deal with. He can't decide whether to stay at Turning Point Ranch with the family he knows and loves.....or move in with his brother Ethan and embrace the inheritance that offers them a prosperous future of their own.

When the world comes crashing down around their ears, they'll all have to come together to make this work before they lose everything all over again.

You can find it at your favorite book retailer.

Get All of AE Moran's Free Books

S ign Up Once—Get all A.E. Moran's free books including brand new releases

Kicked around all his life, alone and penniless, Tom Crenshaw has no choice but to put up with the worst treatment from his sadistic boss, Sawyer Barstow, and Sawyer's equally vicious sons, Cole and Dallas. They treat Tom as less than human, make him sleep on the barn floor, keeping him working all day without food or water, and make him eat on the back steps when they do get around to feeding him.

Only one thing makes Tom's miserable, hopeless existence worthwhile—Sawyer's beautiful daughter, Camille. Too bad she's totally out of reach. Sawyer and his sons would kill Tom just for looking at Camille. She already puts herself in danger by sticking up for him and sneaking him food behind her father's back.

Disaster throws Tom and Camille together until they can no longer deny their feelings for each other. This could lead to a catastrophe that will tear them apart forever--if they even survive it.

They only have one chance at any kind of future together—run for it and leave Turning Point Ranch behind forever. Tom plans to sneak Camille off the ranch under cover of darkness and flee across the country before her father and brothers catch up with him. He'll have to pull off a miracle just to accomplish that much and pray it works before he and Camille both lose everything.

Sign up at www.theomann.com to read it for free

About AE Moran

A.E Moran is the contemporary romance pen name for Theo Mann.

I write 70 books per year—and yes, before you ask, all these books are my original creative work. Nothing written under my name is AI-generated or ghostwritten because I write better than AI and any ghostwriter out there.

People don't read fiction for entertainment or to escape from reality. People read fiction to see their humanity reflected in another person's character and story.

This is my promise to you. When you read my books, you'll see your own humanity reflected in the characters and stories. I take this commitment to my readers very seriously. My books are an intimate form of communication between us. I would never disrespect my readers by turning that over to a machine or another writer. This is my bond between me and you as my reader.

I write 20,000 words per day as my daily work output. If anyone with a public platform would like to challenge me to prove this in a controlled environment, feel free to contact me on this website's contact page.

I worked as a professional ghostwriter for fifteen years. Now I'm going for the Guinness World Record by writing 700 books over the next ten years and 1400 books over the next twenty years, all originally written by me. See my website for the full book list.

I'm also the author of *Proof for the Existence of God* and the *Crimes Against Fiction* blog. You can find all my nonfiction work at www.crimes-against-fiction.com.

If you have a story idea, or if you would like me to explore a series in more depth, or if you'd like me to explore a character by writing a spinoff series about that character or world, leave me a message on my website's contact page. I answer all reader emails, so ask me anything, tell me what you liked and didn't like, and let me know where you'd like your favorite series to go. I would love to hear your ideas and find out what you'd like to read next.

You can find out more at www.theomann.com or at www.authoraemoran.com.

Also by AE Moran (so far)